As easily as she
felt around the wood pile, feeling around for a small log
to use as a weapon. The wolf raised its snout in the air
and sniffed. Terrified, Sophia held her breath, hoping it
wouldn't smell her fear.

Cabin at Crescent Lake

by

Lynne Conrad

Cabin at Crescent Lake

COPYRIGHT © 2022 by Lynne Conrad

Cover Art by *Kim Mendoza*

The Wild Rose Press, Inc.
PO Box 708
Adams Basin, NY 14410-0708
Visit us at www.thewildrosepress.com

Publishing History
First Edition, 2023
Trade Paperback ISBN 978-1-5092-4651-9
Digital ISBN 978-1-5092-4652-6

Published in the United States of America

Dedication

Thank you to
my mom, James and family.
Internal Medicine and Feet First sisters.
Diane, Krista, Ms. Anne, Tish and Craig.
All who encouraged me to follow my dream.

Dr. Jolbert,

How many people could
say they were blessed to have
a great boss and a wonderful
friend? I can!

Love you
Lynne

Prologue

October

"Sophia," Nick called out as he came through the front door, letting it bang shut behind him. Not getting an answer, he shouted louder. He checked for her Camaro, but it was gone. Frowning, he returned to the kitchen and dialed her phone. He heard its ring echo in the house. Where was she and why hadn't she taken her phone? He had given her the phone so he could keep up with her with a GPS app Casey had told him about. Passing through the dining room, he noticed a long white envelope tucked underneath the saltshaker on the table. Next to it was her phone.

He snatched up the envelope and read her hurried writing. Cursing, he wadded the envelope up and threw it across the kitchen and into the empty sink. Slipping his phone back into his pocket, he stormed down the hallway to their bedroom. He flung open the slatted closet doors. Her things were gone except for a pair of sandals and a couple of shirts lying on the floor. After quickly scanning his side of the closet, he started flung his clothes to the floor behind him.. Not only were her things gone, but his duffle bag was gone. Angrily, he punched the closet door with his fist, making a jagged hole in the thin wood. He grabbed his phone and pressed another number as he paced around the room, running his fingers through his hair until the line was answered.

"Hey, Case. It's Nick. Sophia's gone and she has *the* key," he shouted into the phone.

"Are you sure?" Casey yelled in his ear.

"Yeah, I'm sure. Meet me at The Four Spades." Nick shoved the phone back in his pocket and kicked a pair of jeans out of his way as he left.

Chapter One

December

Come as soon as you can. Sophia had received the call from her attorney only a half hour ago. Clenching the steering wheel, she punched the gas and sped across the intersection. She barely missed being clipped by a truck as she drove into the small parking lot and guided her car into the empty space closest to the two-story building's glass entrance. Nervously, she smoothed her hair down and checked herself in the rearview mirror, making sure that she looked okay. She had literally dropped everything and jumped in the car, barely remembering to grab her purse and phone.

Quickly, she looked back over her shoulder, which was her habit now, and walked to the heavy glass doors and pulled them open. She inhaled the now familiar smell of fresh lavender as she stepped inside. She moved across the small lobby to the closed glass window.

"Good morning, Sophia," Rebecca greeted her, sliding open the door and looking up from her computer monitor. She smiled brightly with her ruby red lips as she pushed her black, oval-framed glasses back up her freckled nose. Her curly red hair was pulled back in a braid. Sophia smiled back at her, wishing she could wear red lipsticks as well as Rebecca could.

"Good morning. I received an urgent call from Mr. Danes."

"Yes. He told me you were on your way. He'll be with you shortly."

"Great. Thank you." Sophia was about to turn away when she saw a man walk past Rebecca with a file of papers in his hand. He paused briefly and waved before he went into another office. She had noticed Roman the first couple of times she'd been here. His rugged good looks were hard to miss, from his dark hair and snapping blue eyes to his neatly trimmed beard. His firm, chiseled chest was clearly defined in his tailored shirts. She smiled. She thought back to the day he had introduced himself.

He had taken the seat next to her while she waited for Mr. Danes to return to his office and talked with her after introducing himself with a handshake and a warm smile. Relaxed, his legs crossed, he had amused her with stories about lawyers until Mr. Danes returned and, with a cocked thumb, indicated for him to leave.

Taking a seat on the nearest of the two leather couches, she picked up a magazine, flipped through it, and laid it back down. She tapped her foot and waited. Why had she been called in so soon? Everything had been wrapped up and done except for that final court date with Nick, and she wasn't even sure she had to be there. Thankfully, she didn't have to wait long.

"Sophia." Hearing her name, she looked up as the elderly attorney opened the door separating the hallway from the lobby and called for her in his warm, rich voice. She rose and followed him down a carpeted corridor to the last office on the right. "Please have a seat. I'll be right back," he said, waving a hand at the set of familiar matching chairs.

Sophia took a seat and nervously pulled at a loose thread in her jeans as she looked around the large office. His cherry bookshelf and desk were neat and orderly as usual, lined with law books and the few family photos he had displayed. Orderly and ordinary. Not like her chaotic life now. Here she was, twenty-four years old, and most of her days felt like she was on a carousel that wouldn't stop.

"Ah, here we are." He closed the door behind him, which was unusual since he normally left it open. Sitting down across from her, he placed a thin file on the desk and flipped it open.

"How was your Christmas?"

"As well as could be expected, I guess," she answered, biting her lower lip. She had spent the holiday by herself, turning down an invitation to spend the day with her aunt. It just didn't feel like Christmas to her.

"Sophia, I'm not going to beat around the bush. Nick was bonded out of jail yesterday morning, but he didn't show up for his hearing this morning. A warrant was issued for his arrest along with a BOLO." She grimaced as he shuffled through the papers.

"He was bonded out?"

"Yes, but there's more. A state trooper stopped a car along highway 75 north. The officer was shot." Sophia stiffened. "We have reason to believe Nick did it."

"Is…is the officer dead?"

"No. He's in critical condition, but his prognosis is good. I suspect Nick is headed to Spring City to find you. Sheriff Logan faxed me copies of the bench warrant."

Sophia shuddered.

"Nick was pretty angry when we filed an order of

protection and pressed assault charges against him." Mr. Danes shuffled the papers into a neat pile and placed them back in the plain folder.

"I remember." Sophia nodded and clutched tightly to the seat arm, turning her knuckles white. She could still see Nick's eyes smoldering when he had stared at her across the courtroom, but for the life of her, she couldn't understand why. She concentrated on the judge.

"The police have checked out his known hangouts, but no leads. And the Tennessee Highway Patrol have the BOLO reports too, but unfortunately, the car he was reported to be in was found abandoned, and the make and model of the vehicle he has now is unknown."

"I'm sure his cousin Casey is helping him." Frowning, she began twisting the string on her jeans again. Casey would do whatever Nick wanted him to— for a price. She was as much afraid of Casey as she was of Nick, maybe even more. Casey was evil with no conscience and dark, cold eyes that sent ripples of fear through her. He carried a switchblade inside his belt and never missed a chance to let her know it was there. Whenever he came around, she made sure to never be alone with him.

"We need to talk about keeping you safe until he's back behind bars," he said in his kindly voice, his soft brown eyes watching her. Mr. Danes was an aggressive bear in the courtroom. He was a kind, caring man outside of it.

"What can I do? I keep pepper spray in my purse, but I don't have a gun." Her voice shook as the fear grew inside her.

"You need more protection than that. He almost killed you, not to mention that he threatened to kill you in court, and now he's shot a cop. He's considered armed and very dangerous."

"I know," she whispered, moving her gaze to the office windows. Instinctively, she raised her hand to her throat, vividly remembering the evening that Nick put his hands around her neck, yelling and shaking her, making her feel powerless as she tried to free herself. When he'd let go, she had fallen to her knees, gasping for air. She knew then, without a doubt, that one day he would kill her in one of his rages and that she needed to get away—fast.

"I don't think it will be long before he's back in custody. Is there someone you could stay with?"

"No." Sophia shook her head. Her aunt lived over in Knox County, but if Nick found her there, he might hurt Sylvia too, and she didn't want that. "There's not much I can do. I can't afford to stay at a motel for more than a night or two." Mr. Danes dropped his gaze to the file in front of him. "What happens if they catch him?"

"*When* they catch him, he'll go back to jail with no bond."

She shivered again, twisting her hands together. Nick's threat to kill her echoed in her head. Feeling helpless, she gazed at Mr. Danes with fearful eyes.

"Sophia, the firm has a hunting cabin ten miles outside of Cutbank, Montana. How about we fly you up there to stay until Nick is caught? Mr. and Mrs. Banner, the caretakers, will be there to help you and check on you. You'll have things to keep you comfortable, but remember, it gets quite cold there, along with frequent snowstorms. I'll have Roman fly up there with you. You remember him?"

"Yes."

"Roman's our in-house detective and he's also my nephew. He can be trusted. He has no impending cases he's working on, so he's agreed to go. Rest easy. Of all the staff here, no one but me, Roman, and two senior partners know where the cabin is. You'll be safe."

"I hate for you to go to all that trouble. You really think that Nick will come after me?"

"I have no doubt he'll search for you. He's an evil man. But I'm confident he won't find you there. And as far as being trouble, you're not. I thought a great deal of your dad, and after he and your mom were killed in that awful car accident, I really hurt for you. You looked so vulnerable. There wasn't much I could do for you then, so please let me help you now." Smiling, he folded his hands on his desk. Tears welled up in her eyes, but she quickly blinked them away.

"My dad thought a lot of you, too, but you've already done so much for me with the divorce and getting the judge to sign the papers so quickly, helping me find a job, and an apartment..." She continued to twist her hands in her lap.

"Your dad was one of the most well-liked security guards at the courthouse. He was always telling entertaining stories about growing up in Greece. He did a fine job trying to keep everyone safe. Let me repay that by keeping you safe."

"And you don't think it'll take long to find him?"

"I don't think so, but I can't say for sure. Right now, he's on everyone's radar; however, if he's gone underground for a while..." He shrugged his shoulders and spread his hands. "But for whatever reason, I feel he's coming for you. Just stay as long as you can and give the police time to find him."

"Okay." She sighed. She trusted Mr. Danes. "I'll go. Just tell me when."

"How quickly can you be packed?"

"Less than an hour." She stood up.

"Good. Roman will pick you up at your apartment. He'll be driving a black Camry, a rental. I don't want you to be alone, so I'm sending a police escort home with you, and I'll have Tom, another junior partner, ride with Roman and drive your car back to our storage facility, if that's okay with you?"

"That's fine." She nodded, slowly walking to the door.

"Great. The tickets will be ready when you all get to the airport. I'll take care of the details and contact your employer."

"Thank you." She left, not waiting for him to walk her to the front door as he usually did. He picked up the phone and gave Rebecca instructions to call the airport. A cold wind stung her cheeks and whipped her hair across her face as she climbed into her car.

Chapter Two

Nick scanned the almost deserted parking lot, lit only by two security lights, before he got out of the banged-up, rusted Impala, amazed it hadn't fallen apart on the drive here. Not seeing anything unusual, he pulled his cap down over his eyes and ducked his head as he crossed the cracked parking lot of the old Spring City Motel. He rapped on the metal door. Immediately the door opened, and he stepped inside the musty-smelling room. Casey peered out, scanning the parking lot, and then closed and locked the door. Nick made sure the heavy green drapes were pulled completely shut.

"Did you get everything?" Nick tossed his cap onto the scratched dresser and moved from the window to the micro fridge. He grabbed a beer and sat down in the leather chair next to it, popping the tab. Casey pointed to the red duffle bag on the nearest bed. Casey wasn't the sharpest tool in the shed, but he had connections, and if something was needed, he could get it.

"Yeah, everything's there," Casey said. He sat in the chair opposite Nick, his long legs stretched out and crossed at his ankles. He still had his sunglasses on his head, his black hair pushed back from his face by them.

"Do you know anything about Sophia?" Nick asked.

"No."

"Did you look where I told you to?"

10

"Yep. No luck. She's got a head start on us. The moment you skipped bail, her lawyer knew about it, not to mention the incident with the trooper." Casey sniffed, shrugged, and shook his head all in the same motion. Then he rose from the chair, stretched out his thin arms, and stepped into the bathroom.

Irritated, Nick watched him saunter to the bathroom. He downed the rest of the beer, crumpled the can, and tossed it at the wastebasket, but missed. Her lawyer would no doubt have gotten word about him jumping bail and shooting the trooper from that cagy Sheriff Logan, and she would have been alerted instantly. His question was, had she gone into hiding on her own or did someone, namely that lawyer, help her? What he hadn't counted on was her disappearing so quickly. He should have kept Casey tailing her, but he had needed him to get out of Georgia undetected.

"I wonder…" Nick muttered to himself as he got up to check out the duffle bag. Casey came out of the bathroom and plopped back down in the chair by the micro fridge. "Casey, I wonder, if her lawyer was helping her, where would he hide her? Spring City is a small town, so I wouldn't think around here."

"I don't know, but I can always break into his office and see what I can find," Casey offered, his dark eyes following Nick's movements.

"No, not yet. I have a plan. Besides, I figure they wouldn't keep that kind of information where it could be found. Danes isn't stupid." He dumped the contents of the bag onto the bed. Sifting through the items, he noted the clothes he had asked for, a roll of twenties, a disposable cell phone, a new brown baseball cap, a box of brown hair dye, a wallet, binoculars, a new Glock and ammunition—but most importantly, a new driver's license. Pulling a previously stolen pistol from his waistband, he laid it on the dresser.

"Dispose of this while I'm taking a shower," he said. Then he flipped a twenty onto the dresser next to the gun. "And get us some hot food."

"Anything in particular?"

"Burgers and fries."

After Casey left, Nick grabbed the box of dye and went into the bathroom. When he came out an hour later with a new hair color, Casey was back and sitting at the round table eating. After Nick ate, he repacked the stuff on the bed and picked up his new license to examine it.

"Who am I now?" He turned the card over, reading the name before he tucked it away in the wallet. "Leon Martin."

"The Glock is registered to Leon Martin, too," Casey said, getting up to dump his trash in the garbage can.

"Good. Now I want to rest. We'll leave around dawn." Nick scratched his newly colored beard and pulled off his jeans, laying them across the chair he had just vacated. "By the way, this place you found us to stay at, is it out of the way and low key?"

"Yeah, there's an abandoned shack down at Duncan's River. It's about ten miles outside of town and isolated."

"That'll work."

"You know, Nick, I um, don't understand how you could've been so careless to let her get that key. If she takes it to the cops…" He made a slashing motion across his neck.

Nick swore out loud. The testiness in Casey's voice

and the stress of the last few hours of coming out of hiding himself and crossing state lines boiled over. "She won't," he hissed and then relaxed. "We figured she'd go into hiding as soon as Danes found out about the trooper incident and my not showing up for court. Having to stay underground for a couple weeks gave her a head start, but we'll find her. Trust me. We'll find her."

"Hopefully, but Sophia's not stupid. Timid but not stupid," Casey scoffed. "She'll wonder why a key was hidden in the duffle bag."

"I said I'd take care of it." Nick scowled. But Casey was right about Sophia; he just didn't want to admit it. Nick stared at Casey. His face was red, and he looked as though he wanted to say more but dropped his gaze instead and walked away.

Nick lay down on the bed, closed his eyes, and turned away from Casey, slowing his breathing. He heard the light switch off, leaving only a thin beam of moonlight coming in through the gap of the worn curtains. He lay in the semi-darkness thinking about Sophia and the first time he had laid eyes on her.

Sophia was visiting Stone Mountain with her parents, spreading their blankets on the ground for the laser show, when he spied her a few feet away. He had been sitting cross-legged on a worn quilt with his girlfriend, Gina, sipping beers. Gina was laughing, telling some dumb story that he wasn't listening to. He was watching the slim, auburn-haired beauty as she moved around, helping her parents get ready for the show.

He made some excuse about needing to go to the john and told Gina to stay with their cooler. As he passed by, he slowed to get a good look at the girl with emerald eyes, slim nose, and lips that begged to be kissed. Her porcelain skin was smooth and flawless. He heard her laugh pleasantly at something her father said. Nick casually knelt and pretended to tie his shoe just to get a longer look.

Afterward, he had hurried to the bathroom. When he returned and settled back down on his blanket, Gina glared at him, hissing accusations. He shrugged. He owed Gina nothing, and in defiance of her comments, he pulled out his phone and snapped a picture of the captivating beauty. Gina stomped away in a huff. She was barely out of sight before he had the worn blanket to within a couple feet of Sophia and engaged her in conversation.

Casey was right. She was shy and timid, but smart, and that had been her downfall. He certainly hoped that she didn't know she had the key, and if she did happen to find it, that she didn't figure out what it was for. With that thought, he drifted off to sleep.

****

Drumming his fingers on his chest, Casey lay in the dark listening to Nick snore. He should have known what Sophia was up to and hidden the key better. Casey wasn't so sure that she didn't know that she had it. Sure, she was a beauty, but she was smarter than Nick gave her credit for. If she found the key, she wouldn't just toss it aside. She would wonder about a hidden key and take it straight to that old lawyer of hers. Moving his hand to his side, he lightly tapped his knife, snug in its sheath. He didn't know if Nick could kill her as he had threatened, but he could, and would, if it came down to it. The thought relaxed him, and he closed his eyes, slipping into a dreamless sleep.

Chapter Three

Once Sophia was on the plane, she took the window seat and buckled in. She was nervous, but Roman looked relaxed as he folded his sunglasses and slipped them into his jacket pocket. He buckled himself into the seat next to her and adjusted the headrest. Laying his head back, he closed his eyes.

She had been pleasantly surprised that Mr. Danes was sending him with her to Montana. In the office, he looked attractive in his dress pants and tailored shirts, but today he was wearing jeans, a blue polo shirt that accentuated his blue eyes, and a denim jacket, emphasizing his rugged good looks.

The ride to the airport had taken an hour. For the most part, she was silent, but he had made some small talk.

"Sophia is a beautiful name." He glanced at her, sweeping over her, causing her to blush.

"Thank you. I was named after my dad's mother. My grandparents were Greek."

"Interesting. Did you live in Greece?" He smiled, his blue eyes twinkling.

"No. My grandparents moved to America when my dad was seventeen. Mom and Dad went back to visit once before I was born. I've seen pictures of his family home and the city, Myrina, where he grew up. It is quite beautiful, and their house looked out over the Mediterranean Sea. I have relatives who still live there."

"Maybe after this Nick thing is over, you can go and visit." Sophia looked up surprised. "Uncle Ralph brought me up to speed on my way to pick you up."

Sophia nodded and replied. "Yes, I would love that. It would be great to visit family I only knew through letters Mom and Dad received periodically. From what Mr. Danes said, I don't expect to be in Montana long. Surely Nick will be caught soon."

"True enough," he said, but their conversation ended there when he received a phone call. Apparently, he had made plans for the weekend and was having to explain his sudden trip away on urgent business. She heard the unmistakable tone of irritation creep into his voice as he talked, making her uncomfortable and wish that he hadn't been her escort after all.

Turning toward the oval window, she watched as multicolored luggage was loaded into the belly of the plane, wishing for…what? Normalcy? Her old life? Her mom and dad? Tears threatened for the second time that day, but she blinked them back, concentrating on the luggage rolling up the belt, one piece at a time.

She heard the engines roar and felt movement of the plane as it backed away from the terminal. As they ascended into the air, she gripped the seat arms and watched the earth drop away until the plane leveled out. Inhaling deeply, she relaxed as best as she could.

After the attendants took drink orders, she stole a glance at Roman. He was scrolling through his phone, pausing occasionally. She noticed a faint, half-moon scar under his right eye. When he suddenly turned his head toward her, she quickly dropped her eyes to her lap, a habit quickly learned from living with Nick.

"You can keep talking to me if you want to. I don't usually bite—unless I'm provoked," he joked with a lopsided grin. She shrugged, feeling less uncomfortable with his joke. "But I know that you are a bit shy."

"After your phone call earlier, you seemed annoyed at having to accompany me, so I thought I would leave you to your thoughts."

"Maybe a little annoyed, however, not at you. Besides, how could I tell Uncle Ralph no? I had no pressing work and I love trips to the cabin, and Crescent Lake is gorgeous. Did Uncle Ralph tell you that bison, elk, and moose roam freely around the cabin? And the lake can be seen from the cabin, but only from the second floor."

"I'm looking forward to seeing it." She visualized golden sunsets and moose drinking from the lake.

"I'll take you out to the lake, if you don't mind riding a snowmobile or ATV. We should have a couple of days to sightsee, although I don't think you will have to stay hidden away for long. Nick will be in jail before you know it. Uncle Ralph believes that Nick's anger and aggressiveness will make him careless and that will be his undoing."

"Maybe, if they don't underestimate him," she said more to herself than to Roman. His phone vibrated, and when he swiped the screen, she lay back and closed her eyes, praying that they were right. Nick could be maliciously cunning...

****

Roman turned off the call and gazed at Sophia. He felt a stirring in his heart he hadn't felt in a long time. Way too long. Her long hair had fallen across her face as

17

she slept, giving her a childlike appearance. He had observed her on a few of her visits to the office as she nervously waited in their lobby, even slipping in to chat with her once when she was alone in the office, but Uncle Ralph hadn't needed his help with her case, until now.

She whimpered in her sleep, and feeling like a schoolboy again, he reached out and lightly touched her arm. She was beautiful, and he felt he could drown in her emerald eyes when she looked at him. He knew her situation and what she was facing, and he wanted to protect her. As he watched continued to watch, she whimpered again.

****

"Sophia."

Sophia opened her eyes. Roman was leaning toward her, gently shaking her shoulder. She could feel his lips and warm breath touching her ear.

"What's wrong? I think I dozed off."

"Nothing's wrong. You did doze off. I was going to let you sleep until it was time to descend, but you were whimpering and talking in your sleep," he said, a look of concern on his face. Recalling the dream she had been having about freeing herself from Nick's grasp as he held her by her throat, she felt heat rise in her cheeks and winced.

"I'm sorry."

"Don't be. I figured you were having a nightmare."

"I was." She didn't offer any more information, even as he gave her a knowing look, but changed the subject. "How much longer till we land?"

"About an hour."

"How far is the cabin from the airport?"

"Thirty to fifty minutes, depending on the weather."

For the rest of the flight, she listened to Roman talk about the cabin, the lake, fishing, and hunting, occasionally asking a question.

"By the way, Hill will meet us at the airport to take us up to the cabin."

"Hill?"

"Yeah. Great driver, but a better friend. I've known him for several years. I think you'll like him."

The Fasten Seatbelt sign dinged before he could say anymore, and the plane began its descent toward the blinking lights of the runway. Although dusk was falling, she could still see the jagged, snow-capped mountains surrounding Cutbank.

Fifteen minutes later, the tires hit the tarmac and the plane taxied up to the terminal. She felt Roman's hand on the small of her back as they hurried through the throng of people toward the luggage carousel.

Sophia found her bag and grabbed it up. Roman had just picked his bag up from the circling belt when she heard a deep voice shout out Roman's name. Whirling around, she saw a tall, slim man wearing a leather aviator's hat with brown fur on the inside and a worn bomber's jacket. He was standing next to the exit and waving a long arm in the air. Grinning broadly, Roman waved back, and when the two men met, they hugged, beating each other on the back, laughing like two schoolboys.

"Sophia, this is Hill. Hill—Sophia."

"Nice to meet you." She shook his hand. For someone who had slim hands, he had a strong grip.

"By the way, it's beginning to snow, so we better head out. Forecast is calling for one of our famous snowstorms," Hill informed them as he took her bag with a large grin.

"I was hoping the forecast was wrong," Roman remarked.

"Sorry, pal." Hill led the way through the sliding glass doors and stepped outside.

Chapter Four

Sophia walked quickly beside Roman. Shivering in the sharp, snowy wind, she held her jacket tightly around her. Pointing out a black four-wheel truck, Hill led them to the vehicle. While Roman secured the bags in the back, Hill climbed into the driver's seat and brought the engine to life. He extended a hand to help Sophia into the blessed warmth of the cab. Apparently, he hadn't been waiting at the terminal for very long since the truck still had some heat blowing from the vents.

Smiling, he held her hand longer than she thought he should have. She tugged her hand from his and shoved it into her jacket pocket. With the luggage tied down in the back, Roman slid into the truck beside her. Sophia scooted close to him.

"So, Sophia, hanging out with this guy?" Hill asked, maneuvering through the crowded parking lot toward the exit, the windshield wipers swishing back and forth. Sophia blushed, realizing that Hill didn't know her true purpose for being here. Evidently, he thought she was Roman's girlfriend.

"Sophia, are you comfortable?" Roman asked, saving her from having to answer Hill, but she heard him chuckle as he turned right out of the parking lot and onto the main road. Soon they had left the lights of Cutbank behind them. She watched the snow as it cascaded in the headlights of the truck and listened to the conversation of the men.

Nervously, she twisted the seatbelt after they left the main road, but Roman reached over and squeezed her hand. "Hill's driven in much worse conditions. It'll be fine." He leaned close to whisper in her ear. His breath tingled on her neck. Sophia nodded, embarrassed that her fear was that apparent, but she still held to the seatbelt. She hadn't seen this much snow since she was a little girl.

It had taken a little over an hour to reach their destination, due to the weather, but the men had talked nonstop about everything from hunting and fishing to town gossip. When Hill had turned off the highway, the last seven miles had been a two-lane road leading through dense woods. Finally, she saw a glowing, welcoming light shining through the darkness as the truck rolled to a stop in front of a cabin.

Roman helped her down from the truck, and while he and Hill got the bags, she looked around. The cabin was two levels with a long wooden porch. Firewood was neatly stacked at one end of the porch. The front door was made of a heavy thick wood with three cross planks, but she wasn't sure what it was. Maybe oak.

Behind her, on the other side of the driveway, she glimpsed a large metal shed set at the edge of the tree line. "Let's go," Roman said. Shivering, she followed Roman up the two steps and onto the porch, waiting patiently for him to unlock the door.

Roman pushed open the heavy door, and she stepped into the warm room, followed by the men. Just to her right was a fireplace built from fieldstone. Drawn to the leaping flames, she held out her hands to the inviting glow.

"Wonderful, Otis built a fire for us," Roman said, also holding his hands out to the warmth. Sophia noticed that he had strong, smooth hands but smiled at his well-manicured nails. The two men in her life had rough hands and chipped nails. Her father had worked for years in factories until he got the job at the courthouse three years ago. Nick also had rough hands, but his weren't from hard work.

"Otis?" she asked, slipping away from the fire for a moment to hang her jacket on one of the silver hooks by the door. She hurried back to the fire.

"Otis and his wife Helen are the caretakers. They live about four miles past the cabin." Roman shrugged off his jacket, hanging it beside hers. He picked up his bag and headed up the wide staircase, followed by Hill, who had hers.

Enjoying the warmth of the fire, she studied the small, cozy cabin. The living room and kitchen were separated by a wall, and thick wooden rafters crossed the ceiling. A braided rug lay in front of the hearth. Two identical rocking chairs were placed at each side of the hearth, and a brown leather couch faced the glowing flames in the fireplace. A red and black jacquard throw was neatly folded across the back of the couch, and a matching throw pillow lay against the arm. Above the mantel, a majestic moose head with a large set of antlers hung, completing the room's rustic look.

The staircase that the men had dashed up was wide and led to the second story landing and three rooms that she could see. The first door to the left on the landing was closed. Must be a bedroom that wasn't needed, she thought.

Next to her, a simple bookcase had been built into the recess between the hearth and the staircase and was filled with rows of hardback and paperback books. A wicker basket sat on the floor at its base, filled with magazines. Sophia had been reading since she could hold a book and reading out loud to her mom. She would check out the titles and see what was stashed away on the shelves later.

The kitchen was small and simple, with only the bare necessities and basic appliances. Despite all that had brought her here, she loved the cozy, little cabin. She was rocking slowly in the rocker facing the stairs when she heard Hill's boots thudding down the steps. She looked up, watching as he paused on the last step.

"Hope I put your luggage in the right room." Before she could answer, he winked at her and then sniffed the air dramatically. "Hey, is that homemade muffins I smell?" He hopped off the step and headed toward the kitchen.

"I'm sure they are, and I'll bet they're blueberry. We just have to find where Helen left them," Roman said, following Hill down the steps and into the kitchen. After a short hunt, Roman found them wrapped in a towel and stuffed into a large moose head cookie jar. "Here they are," he called out, spreading the muffins on the table. The sweet blueberry smell reminded Sophia that she hadn't eaten in several hours. "Better get one before Hill wolfs them all down," Roman called out to her.

Timidly, she walked to the table, took one of the golden-brown muffins, and retreated to the fire. She rocked and ate as the two men talked and laughed until Hill announced that he had better leave while he still could.

"Why don't you just crash on the couch?" Roman asked, following him to the door.

"I promised to take Jasper to Donovan's to pick up some truck parts early in the morning."

"How's Jasper doing?" Roman asked. Sophia noticed an edge in Roman's voice.

"Good. He's doing okay."

"All right. I'll see you in the morning."

"I'll be here to pick you up. Should be around nine."

"I'll be ready." Roman patted Hill on the back as he stepped out the door and into the darkness. Sophia shivered from the blast of cold air that whizzed through the door. She heard the truck start and watched as the lights turned back down the road. The snow had stopped, but a thick layer lay on the ground Sophia saw before Roman shut and locked the door behind him.

"Before I forget to tell you, watch as you go in and out this door." He cocked his thumb at it. "Although it has a lock and key, we also have this old-fashioned latch. Uncle Ralph likes it and refuses to take it off the door. Sometimes when the door is shut, it falls into its cradle. It usually stays up with the nail, but accidents have happened. Should you get locked out though, the key also opens the kitchen door." She nodded.

"And last but not least, thankfully, we don't have to rely on the fireplace for warmth. Uncle Ralph also had central heat and air put in a couple years ago. He said the cold was getting too much for his old bones. The thermostat is located just on the other side of the staircase, next to the laundry room," he said, pointing in its direction.

"Okay," she replied, making a mental note not to forget what he said, especially about the door.

"Make yourself at home," he continued, but she could feel him staring at her. Although the air was cool in the room, he made her palms sweat.

"Thank you, I will. I think I'll sit here for a while to watch the fire."

"Yeah, go ahead."

Sophia sat in the cushioned rocking chair facing the door and gently rocked. Roman sat down on the end of the couch and rested his feet on a small footstool. She felt a peaceful calm descend as she stared into the flames.

"I love the fireplace," she suddenly exclaimed. "There was a small one in the house we lived in in Fork Valley when I was a young girl, but we only lived there for a few months." Sophia didn't tell him that they had moved around a lot before finally settling down in Spring City. Her dad, Kostas, had a hard time holding down a job. He was a jovial man with a great personality, and people were drawn to him—when he wasn't drinking. Unfortunately, the bottle frequently kept him unemployed—until they settled in Spring City, and he was hired for a security guard position at the courthouse.

He made a promise to Sophia and her mother, Evie, to stay away from the bottle, and he did, or so Sophia thought. Evie would often tell Sophia how well Kostas was doing at his job and staying sober. But on the night of the accident, a bottle was found under the driver's seat.

An ember crackled loudly, and red sparks flew up the chimney, bringing Sophia back to the present. When she looked up, Roman was gazing at her. Feeling a bit embarrassed, she rose and announced that she was tired and going to bed.

"I'll show you to your room." Roman jumped up

and led the way up the stairs. On the landing, he pointed at the shut door. "That's Uncle Ralph's room. And this is my room." He pointed out the second room as they continued toward the third room on the landing. Just past her bedroom door, a family picture hung on the log wall. She paused at the door to study the picture of a man, a woman, and a young boy against the backdrop of a wooded area.

"Is that you?" she asked, looking at the curly-headed boy.

"Yeah, that's me, Uncle Ralph, and Aunt Marion."

"Nice picture."

"Thank you. This is your room. You have a private bath and everything you need should be in there, but if there is anything you need, let me, Otis, or Helen know." She nodded, suddenly very tired. He turned to leave but paused when she touched his muscled arm.

"Yes," he said, raising his eyebrows.

"Thank you for everything."

"You're welcome." He bounded down the steps but hesitated on the last step, calling back up to her.

"I may be gone when you get up in the morning. Hill's going to take me into Cutbank for some supplies. Is there anything you need?"

"I can't think of anything."

"By the way, I almost forgot to tell you that cell service out here is not good. Actually, it's almost nonexistent, but every once in a while you can catch a break." She waved in acknowledgment and entered the bedroom, locking the door behind her. That night, she slept deeply without nightmares for the first time in a very long time.

Chapter Five

In the early morning hours, just before the sun came up, Nick followed Casey's black S10 to the abandoned cabin on Duncan's River, ten miles outside Spring City. Again he wondered if his clunker would stay together on the bumpy road until they arrived at the dilapidated cabin. The sun was peeking over the low mountain range that surrounded the area when they pulled up to the wooden porch that had collapsed on one end.

"Certainly out of the way," Nick muttered and frowned, surveying the cabin.

"Best I could do on short notice." Casey shrugged and jumped up on the porch. He pushed open the door, which was barely hanging on, and disappeared inside.

Nick followed him, careful where he stepped on the rotted porch. The inside wasn't much better. A fireplace was set into the wall to his left, but the mantel was hanging down, held on by a rusted nail. A broken table lay scattered in the far corner to his right, but the sink was still standing and in working order. Casey had two makeshift cots set up, one on each side of the fireplace.

While Casey moved around the cabin and gathered the broken pieces of a table to start a fire, Nick placed his duffle bag on the cot nearest the door. Sorting through it, he pulled out a large brown envelope and laid it aside on the floor next to the cot. Next, he pulled out a clean shirt and hung it on a nail he saw sticking out of the wall, along with his new cap. Afterward, he lay down and rested for a couple of hours. When he got up, he looked around to find Casey gone. He changed his clothes and went out to hunt for him. He found him sitting on the riverbank, fishing.

"I have to run an errand. When I get back, I'll let you know what our next move is."

"Sure, but what if we can't find her? What if she *does* find the key? What if she figures it out?" Casey asked coldly, staring Nick in the eye.

"For the last time, she won't, and I will find her," Nick growled, fighting the urge to punch Casey. He strode to his car and sped away toward Spring City and his destination: the law office of Danes and Associates.

****

The parking lot of Lance's Pharmacy was directly across the street from the law firm. Nick parked the Impala between a black van and a Ford F-150 and waited. He had toyed with the idea of just breaking into the office, but Danes wasn't a dumb cluck. Any information of Sophia's whereabouts would be nonexistent, no doubt. Force wouldn't work either, he thought. He continued to watch and go over his plan until cars began to pull into the parking lot across from him.

Grabbing up a pair of binoculars, he watched the well-dressed women stroll into the building, talking to each other and carrying coffee cups, but one in particular caught his attention. He focused the binoculars on her. She was his target.

Rebecca. A tall, slim redhead. Black-framed glasses and thin red lips. Her black dress, partially hidden under a short jacket, curved with her body, and her black flats were a perfect match to the dress. He watched as she looked behind her and waved at a car that honked as it sped past her. Then she stepped into the office.

He waited about ten minutes before he crossed the street to the brick building Rebecca had entered. Pulling his cap low, he swung open the heavy glass door and approached the window, holding the envelope up as though he were reading a name. Rebecca sat behind the window, adjusting her computer screen. Patiently he waited until she slid open the window.

"May I help you?" she asked in a flat voice, but when she looked up, he saw her eyebrows raise, and her voice softened when she continued talking. "Do you have an appointment?"

"Hi. No, I don't have an appointment. I'm looking for..." he paused, pretending to read the name on the envelope. "Sarah Howell."

"I'm sorry. There's no one here by that name." Rebecca frowned. Something he already knew.

"Oh. I guess I wrote the address down wrong."

"Do you know where she works, or the place you were supposed to deliver it to? Maybe I can help."

"Nah, I told my friend's mom I would deliver it for her since I was coming to town. I'll call him and get the correct address." He waved the envelope in the air.

"You're welcome to use my phone."

"That's okay. I've got his number in my cell phone in the car, but uh, I am glad that I got the wrong address."

"Really? Why is that?" Rebecca asked, raising her eyebrows again.

"Because I believe I just ran into the prettiest girl in town." Nick watched her cheeks turn bright red. He grinned and leaned closer into the window. Her blue eyes were the only pretty features she possessed, he thought. Her nose was slightly crooked, and her thin lips covered a small overbite. She wore extra mascara to hide the fact that her eyelashes were short and thin. He was probably the only man to ever tell her she was pretty. "What's your name?"

"Rebecca. Rebecca Sawyer."

"Nice to meet you, Rebecca Sawyer."

"Nice to meet you, uh, Mr.…"

"Martin, Leon Martin."

"Nice to meet you, Mr. Martin, but if there's nothing else I can help you with, I need to get back to work. Want to keep the boss man happy, you know." She chuckled lightly.

He turned as though he were leaving, then hesitated and moved back to the window. "Actually, Ms. Sawyer, I would like to ask you to have dinner with me. That is, if you aren't in a relationship already?" He doubted she had any boyfriends.

"I don't know you, so I don't think so."

"Okay, how about we meet somewhere and have a drink? Get to know each other." He knew he was halfway home with her when she hesitated while looking him over.

"All right. Tomorrow night at Dale's Grille, down at the end of Willow Avenue, say about seven. We'll see how it goes," she finally answered. "Do you know where it is?"

"Yeah."

"Great, and you can call me Becky. By the way, they do line dancing on Friday nights, so wear your dancing shoes."

"I'll be there," he replied as the window closed and

31

she picked up the phone. Walking out, he chuckled to himself. He was on his way to finding the key.

Chapter Six

Morning broke with a dull, overcast sky. Snow was softly falling, clinging to the windowpanes as the flakes fell against them. Shivering, Sophia threw back the blue comforter and dashed to the bathroom. After showering, she dressed and hurried down the stairs, but gasped, pausing at the bottom. A large man was squatting on the hearth, pitching pieces of dry wood into the crackling fire and humming a tune she didn't recognize. Standing up, he turned toward her, dusting the ash off his hands on his blue overalls. He was roughly sixty years old, six feet tall, and had wavy gray hair and a matching grizzled beard. He smiled broadly when he saw her.

"Ah, you must be Sophia," he said, holding out a large hand to her, but, taken aback, Sophia stepped back up the stairs, both hands on the banister. Her eyes darted around for Roman, but not seeing him, she remembered that he had been supposed to leave with Hill this morning. She was about to flee up the stairs when the large man, seeing the look of fear on her face, dropped his hand and moved backward to the fire, a slight frown on his face.

"I'm Otis, and the beautiful woman in the kitchen is my wife, Helen. We're the caretakers." He pointed to the slim, silver-haired woman taking a pan of biscuits from the oven. Sophia shifted her gaze to the petite woman bustling around the kitchen. "I'm sorry for startling you, but didn't Roman tell you we would be here?"

"I guess I forgot," she answered, relieved. Roman had even mentioned Helen last night. Giving Otis a timid smile, she stepped forward to shake his calloused hand when he offered it a second time.

"Hi, Sophia. I hope we didn't wake you up. We were trying to be quiet." Helen's cheery voice rang out from the kitchen as she set the pan of biscuits on the table.

"Oh no, you didn't. I actually meant to get up earlier, but I was so tired I slept longer. Did you see Roman this morning?"

"No, he was already gone when we arrived, but I'm sure he'll be back soon," Otis replied, walking up behind her. "But there's a snowstorm in the forecast, so Helen and I will probably get things done up and leave early."

"Okay." Sophia nodded. "What do I need to do to help?" Moving toward the stove, she smiled at Helen. She knew she already liked the couple and Helen's warm, sweet smile.

"Just sit down at the table and get ready to eat. I hope you like country ham, eggs, and gravy with biscuit."

"I do." Sophia laughed lightly, her stomach growling from the smoky smell of the ham still sizzling in the pan.

"Otis, be a dear and get the jam from the refrigerator, please." Sophia watched as his large frame leaned into the fridge, pushing jars around until he found the jam and set it on the table. Then he took a seat next to Sophia.

"Okay, Helen, we are ready to eat." Otis chuckled and smacked the table with his fork. Sophia giggled softly as Helen set out the food.

"Ya'll dig—" Helen began but paused when the

front door blew open and a snowy figure stepped inside, stomping snow from his boots. When he had shed his coat and boots, Roman hurried to the kitchen in his stocking feet.

"Roman!" Helen cried out when he grabbed her in a bear hug and swung her around. When her feet were on the floor again, he grabbed Otis's hand, shaking it and hugging him all at the same time.

"You're just in time for breakfast," Helen said, pointing Roman to a chair.

"I know. I could smell that ham from a mile away." He sat down and turned to Sophia, winking at her. She smiled shyly at him and bit into a piece of ham.

"How are Ralph and Marion doing?" Helen asked, sitting beside Roman.

"Everyone's doing well. I'll tell them you asked."

"Tell him I'm looking forward to a hunting trip again," Otis said through a mouthful of biscuit. "Looks like we're going to having some deep snowfalls this year, good hunting weather."

"Certainly looks like it, although I was hoping it wouldn't get bad so I could show Sophia some of the sights."

"The snowmobiles will go when other vehicles won't, and they're already gassed up."

"Sophia, more ham, dear?" Helen held the plate while Sophia helped herself. She ate slowly while listening to the men talk about the cabin, fishing, and hunting. Helen, catching a pause in their conversation, took over to ask Sophia about herself.

"Do you have any family?"

"I have an aunt living in Knoxville, but my parents died in an accident. No brothers or sisters."

"I'm so sorry, dear."

"Thank you. It happened two years ago," Sophia added. Helen patted her hand.

"Do you have hobbies? If you like to read, there are lots of books here."

"I do like to read. And I play piano, but my real passion is painting." Sophia felt her cheeks flush when she looked around to see Roman was gazing intently at her.

"That's wonderful. I bet you're very good at it. What kind of pictures do you paint?" Helen continued.

"I don't know how good I am at it, but I like painting nature scenes, animals, and sometimes people."

"And you play piano too? I had an aunt that played. She could make the piano hop around the floor." Otis injected.

"I love music. Mom and I danced around the living room to all kinds of music." Sophia could still envision her mom swirling on the braided rug, holding her small hands in hers. "I guess that love of music is what inspired me to learn the piano."

Helen was smiling at her with a faraway look in her eyes.

"Ah, I remember Otis and me dancing the nights away to the music of Elvis, The Big Bopper, and Chubby Checker at Nero's Diner."

"And don't forget Roy Orbison's "Pretty Woman." Whenever I heard it on the radio, I always thought of you, dear. Those were some good times," Otis recalled with a chuckle.

"Maybe you two could give us dance lessons." Roman laughed, taking a bite of ham. Sophia liked his light-hearted laugh. It made her think of her father's.

"I bet we could show you a few slick moves. We were awesome on the dance floor. Even won a couple of dance contests," Helen quipped, turning her attention back to Sophia. "Otis and I will be out to check on you and help in any way we can. I will help with the cooking, but feel free to cook anything you like."

"Uh, cooking's not one of my strong points." Sophia bit her lip, remembering Nick pitching food into the trash can, shouting about it being overcooked or tasting bad. She could never please him.

"I'm sure you are a fine cook, but there are a few things in the freezer ready to thaw and warm up, just in case the weather turns foul, and we can't get out here for a couple of days." Sophia nodded. "If you do need anything, just tell Roman to let me know, or you can try to call. Both our cell phone numbers are stuck on the fridge door under the cow magnet. I included our landline number, although the cabin doesn't have one."

"Thank you. I'm sure I'll be fine. I don't expect to have to stay very long."

"But if I may ask, when is your baby due?" Helen asked, smiling as she cleared the table. Sophia quickly glanced over at Roman, who was staring at her with a glass of juice halfway to his open mouth, but she quickly dropped her head, feeling her cheeks flush hot and tears welling up in her eyes. She didn't know what to say. She had told no one about her pregnancy, not even Nick. She had just found out she was pregnant when she left him. Instinctively, she dropped her hand to her belly and looked up into Helen's soft brown eyes.

"I'm, um, not really sure," she whispered, her voice quivering. A tear rolled down her cheek.

"I'm so sorry. I've upset you," Helen spoke softly,

taking Sophia's hand.

"No, really, I'm okay. But how did you know?"

"I can just tell. My grandmother was Navajo, and I inherited many of her intuitions. Besides, I noticed you caressing your stomach a couple of times."

"I didn't even realize I was doing—"

"Excuse me," Roman interrupted, leaving the table to sprint up the stairs.

"Well, where's he going in such a hurry?" Otis asked, getting up to put more logs on the fire. Helen only shook her head and finished clearing the table. Nervously, Sophia wondered about Roman too.

When the dishes were done and the wood box filled, Otis and Helen left with strict orders to call them or send Roman out if she needed anything. When they were gone, she drifted over to the fireplace, settling down on the couch to watch the dancing flames. She thought about the house her family had lived in with the fireplace. She would take the poker and jab at the logs to make the embers crackle and fly up the chimney. Although her mom had warned her not to do it, she had anyway—until her hand had slipped, and she had been burned. She still had the scar on her pinky finger.

Trying to relax, she visualized her mom, Evie. Always loving, eager to cuddle with her at bedtime or reading stories to her. Eventually her memories turned dark, about Nick and the pain he had caused pushed through. Her thoughts were interrupted when she heard Roman coming down the steps. She took a deep breath, not sure what he would say.

"Hey, are you okay?" He sat down beside her, his knee touching hers. His hair was still wet from showering, and she could smell his aftershave.

"I, uh, don't know. I guess so." She exhaled slowly, relieved by the kindness in his voice.

"Sorry I left the table abruptly, but I was so surprised about your news that I spilt juice down my shirt and my pants. I left to clean up." He chuckled softly. "Does Uncle Ralph know?" He gazed at her with gentle eyes. She shook her head, twisting the hem of her shirt.

"I didn't want anyone to know. Especially Nick. It's wrong, I know, but I just want him out of my—our life." She felt she needed to explain herself.

Roman scooted off the couch to squat in front of the fire. He ran his hand through his hair and scratched at his beard as he stared at the leaping orange-red flames. Sophia sat quietly, gazing at his muscular back and arms. After several minutes, he sat back down beside her.

"Uncle Ralph will have to be told." Sophia nodded. "I can't imagine what happened between you and Nick, but we'll keep you safe. How did he get bonded out anyway?"

Sophia shrugged. "His cousin Casey probably came up with the money, but Mr. Danes was surprised he was even given bail."

"I am too. But squeaky lawyers and money can do a lot of things. Having shot a trooper, though, he'll be hunted like a dog. Tomorrow I'll try to contact Uncle Ralph and see if there's been any news."

"Okay and thank you again."

"Sophia, you realize that your secret may have to be told?" She bit her lip. Despite the warmth of the cabin, she shivered at the thought of Nick knowing about the baby. "But with Nick's past and the allegations against him, I don't think there will be any problems with child custody."

She sighed, relieved.

"And I will talk to Dr. Rader on my next visit to town and see if he can check on you periodically if it turns out that you're here for a while." Roman reached over and squeezed her hand.

"Okay." She slowly smiled at him. Roman had shown more kindness in the last few minutes than Nick had in their whole marriage.

"I'm going to take the snowmobile to Otis's and get some things from the shed. I'll be back in about two hours. Do you want to go?"

"No, I'm good. I think I'll rest or read while you're gone."

When he had donned his parka, boots, and gloves, he headed out. Sophia went to the window adjacent to the fireplace and watched him leave. She had told Helen that she knew where everything was, but that had been a half-truth. She roamed around the cabin to get more familiar with it, checking out the pantry, the rooms, except for Roman's, and the books on the shelves. When the fire died down, she threw more logs on it, causing the flames to leap and dance. After making a cup of hot chocolate, she settled in front of the cozy fire, sipping the chocolate until she drifted off to sleep.

****

Roman sped toward Otis and Helen's on the snowmobile, much faster than he knew he should, but he was troubled at the events that had just unfolded. Uncle Ralph would have to know about the child, but he could see in Sophia's eyes the fear she had of Nick. He felt a surge of anger toward Nick. There was only a pistol at the cabin, but he had a rifle packed away in the shed. He made a mental note to get the pistol from the safe and make sure that Sophia knew how to load and shoot it. Just in case.

Chapter Seven

Waking early, Nick rose and stretched. He glanced over at Casey, who was still sleeping, his blanket pulled over his head. He splashed water on his face and then looked for the cooler. It was stashed beside Casey's cot. He fished out a water, took a cinnamon roll from the package on the makeshift table, and strolled down to the water's edge, where he sat down on a log.

He picked up a smooth stone and rubbed it between his fingers, his thoughts turning to Sophia. Had he been in love with her? No, but she was a beauty he had wanted to own. Marrying her was the only way he could have her. She had asked the usual questions about his life and family, but he had answered most of them with lies. He didn't tell her about his first marriage. She didn't need to know. His dad was in prison for armed robbery, and his mom had taken up with a truck driver and was living somewhere in Texas, but he told her they were dead.

He had believed that her shy, unassuming ways would keep her quiet and out of his business, but it had only taken a few weeks for him to realize that she was sharper than he had given her credit for.

"But not this time, baby, not this time," he muttered. Rising from the log, he skipped the stone across the river, watching it until it slid beneath the surface.

He pulled a piece of soap from his pocket, stripped,

and waded out into the river. Hurriedly, he bathed and grabbed up his clothes, walking naked into the cabin. Casey was sitting on the edge of the cot, his head in his hands. Nick dressed and grabbed a razor from his bag.

"Casey, I need a better car," Nick said, trimming and adding more dye to his beard in front of a broken piece of mirror he had found lying in a corner.

"I'll see what I can do. But what's wrong with that one?" He pointed his finger toward the Impala.

"I have a date tonight, and I don't want to show up in that thing."

"You have a what?" Casey looked at him incredulously.

"A date."

"Really? Do you think that's wise?"

"It's fine. It's not for fun. I need a car that won't stand out. I need something that people wouldn't look at twice." Nick glared at Casey. He was tired of him questioning his plans. "And dump the Impala somewhere."

"What time do you need it by?"

"Yesterday."

"Okay. Give me a few minutes to locate something," Casey muttered, and picking up the keys, he was out the door and driving away in the Impala.

****

Casey drove the Impala at breakneck speed up the dirt road toward town, cursing under his breath. Why couldn't Nick just do this the easy way? Yeah, they had to be careful, but he could break into the office, find what they needed, and no one would be the wiser. The problem with Nick was he always wanted to do things his way, like shooting the trooper. "Had to be done,"

Nick said, but Casey knew Nick had enjoyed shooting him.

Grimacing, Casey remembered his mom saying that Nick was just like his dad, mean and controlling. Casey could handle the mean, but the controlling…

When he turned out onto the highway, he picked up his cell phone and made a call.

****

Two hours later, Nick heard a car come down the gravel drive. Cracking the door open, his hand on his pistol, he peered out at the silver Altima pulling up to the porch. Casey was behind the wheel, smiling like a fat cat. He opened the door and jumped out.

"How's this?"

"Sweet, but I don't want any details about how you got it." Nick jumped off the rotted porch to check the car out. He had to admit that Casey had done well. It was perfect—low key and respectable. "Now there's just a couple more things."

"Yeah, what?"

"First, I will need more cash in a couple of days. Second, we know Sophia's fat lawyer has already told her about my jumping bail and the trooper incident. After my unintentional outburst in the courtroom, I'm sure they'll all believe I'm after her. What I don't know is if she's hiding on her own or if her lawyer has whisked her away?"

"What's the difference?"

"I figure if she's hiding on her own, she'll be close because she has limited funds, as far as I know. But if her lawyer is helping her, and I believe he is, well, his deep pockets could send her anywhere, even out of the country. That's what I'm gonna find out.

"Sophia also had a coworker she was fairly close to before we moved to Georgia. Nikki Swan. I want you to check her out, make sure that Sophia's not with her. Here's the address—but be careful. Nikki lives alone, but she does have a German shepherd that's loud and aggressive." Nick shoved a folded piece of paper at him. Casey took the paper, chewing on his lower lip, and shoved it in his pocket.

"Did you get rid of the Impala where it won't be found?"

"It's in the river."

"Good."

"You know, there's something I want to ask. It's been bugging me."

"What is it?" Nick muttered. He could tell something was eating at Casey, and he bet he knew what it was.

"Why didn't you put that key in a safe place? Remember I said we should make a second copy." Casey asked, his voice tinged with irritation. "How much do you think she knows? And you know how dangerous it is for her to have it."

"I thought it was in a safe place and yeah, maybe we should have made a second copy." Nick stared at Casey, reining in his irritation. Casey had as much riding on that key as he did, and he had a right to be angry. But Nick was angrier at himself—more than anyone else was—for not guarding it better. Obviously, he had underestimated Sophia, but it wouldn't happen again. The only hope he had was that she didn't know about the key or find it.

"I'll take care of it, and I will find it."

Shaking his head, Casey threw his hands up and strolled to the back of the cabin. After a few moments,

Nick watched as he drove away in his truck, then he rested until it was time to leave for his date. He lay and plotted his moves with Rebecca. Afterward his mind turned to Sophia and the key. Had she found it? Hopefully not. Would she even know what it was for? Maybe not, but still, he wondered…

He fell asleep. When he awoke, Casey still wasn't back. He checked the time, then finished dressing and slipped into the Altima, heading to Dale's Grille.

Chapter Eight

It was early afternoon when Sophia opened her eyes. It was quiet in the cabin. She rose up, stretched and noticed the fire had died down. After throwing a couple pieces of wood on the fire, she went upstairs to grab her phone, wondering if she had any service. As she left her room to go back down, she peeked into Roman's room. It was empty, but his bed was an unmade mess. She laid her phone aside and made the bed, making sure the corners were tight, the way Nick had made her do it. Then she gathered up his dirty clothes, took them to the laundry room, and threw them in the washer.

Leaning against the washing machine, she sighed deeply. Despair overwhelmed her, and she wondered if her memories and fear of Nick would ever fade. Could she be strong enough for herself and the baby? She caressed her stomach. She would do everything she could to take care of her child, but in the back of her mind, she knew some memories would be there for a long time to come.

Her stomach rumbling with hunger brought her out of reverie and she saw it was three-thirty. She made a sandwich and took it to the couch to eat. Before she sat down, she took the poker and stirred up the fire, watching the fiery embers float up the chimney. She wondered where Roman was. It wasn't her business and she wouldn't ask when he came back.

"Darn, I forgot my drink." Sophia groaned out loud and went back to the kitchen. She wished Helen were there to talk to—not to tell her troubles to, but for her company. Sophia hoped she would be back before long. She was reaching for the pitcher of tea when she heard the cabin door open and Roman call out.

Looking around the corner, she saw him set a couple of boxes on the floor and shrug out of his parka and boots. His nose and cheeks were a bright red. "Sophia, where are you?"

"I'm here in the kitchen." She got the ham back out and made him a sandwich. "Do you prefer mustard or mayo?" she asked when he sat down at the table.

"Hey, thanks, but you don't have to make sandwiches for me. I've been making my own since I was five. Mom would laugh at the way I made peanut butter and jelly sandwiches."

"And why was that?" Sophia placed the sandwich on a plate and set it in front of him.

"I put peanut butter on one slice of bread and jelly on the other and then smash them together like this." He demonstrated, bringing an unbidden smile to her lips.

"I guess everyone has their own way. Do your parents live in Tennessee, too?" she asked. A shadow crossed his face, and he momentarily looked away toward the fire. "I'm sorry. You don't have to answer that."

She heard him sigh as he looked back at her. "It's okay. Really. My parents died when I was nine. Uncle Ralph and Aunt Marion took me in. They were not able to have children of their own, and they adopted me. They put me through college and law school, and then Uncle

Ralph gave me a job at the firm."

"I'm sorry for your loss, but Mr. Danes is such a great man," Sophia replied, thinking about the good things he had done for her. "Being a lawyer must be an interesting job."

"Although I passed the bar and can practice law, I prefer the challenge of working as a detective. And you're right. Uncle Ralph is a great guy."

"My parents died in a car accident." She felt a pang of hurt at the memories of the phone call from the sheriff and of trying to get to Tennessee as Nick decided there was no need to hurry since they were already dead. He let her stay for the funeral and then only long enough to get the death certificate. They came back one more time when her parents' small house was sold. Nick spent the money gambling as soon as she received the check.

Nick hated her parents, especially her dad, because they had seen what she hadn't— that he was a man with a dark heart and soul. Her father hadn't hidden his feelings, although her mom tried to keep the peace between them. Sophia had concealed from them how bad Nick really was. After the funeral, the only thing Nick asked was if they had any money in the bank she would inherit. She shuddered at the memory.

"I'm sorry too, Sophia. At least I had family to turn to, while you didn't really have anyone, did you?"

"No, I didn't."

"Hey, I'll be right back." He bounded up the stairs to his room. When he came back down, he was carrying her phone and laid it beside her.

"Thank you," he said, frowning. Sophia caught the frown and froze with the pitcher of tea in midair as she was about to refill his glass.

"What's wrong? Did you want something else?" she asked, feeling the familiar prickling of fear.

"Nothing's wrong. I'm just not used to someone waiting on me or making my bed."

"I'm sorry."

"You don't have anything to be sorry about. It's okay, but you don't have to do that." He bit into his sandwich. Mustard clung to his upper lip, and he wiped it away with his hand.

"I'm sor...uh, okay." She took her glass to the fireplace and sat down on the couch, staring into the flames. She looked back over her shoulder when she heard Roman shouting into his phone. Apparently he had gotten service.

Sipping her tea, she wondered if she had upset him by going into his room. She hadn't meant any harm, and it was just to make up the bed. She wished again her mom were here. Helen's warm personality reminded Sophia a great deal of her mom. She brushed away a tear as it trickled down her cheek. She was deep in thought when Roman spoke to her again, causing her to jump and almost spill the glass of tea. He was standing directly behind her, but she hadn't heard him walk up.

"Service wasn't good. Mostly static. I hope Hill understood that I wanted him to take me back to town tomorrow for ammunition."

"I'm sorry. I know you don't want to hang out with me all the time," she whispered barely loud enough for him to hear, but inside she wasn't sorry at all.

"Oh, no, that's not the case at all. I wanted more ammo and thought I would take you along if you wanted to go and see the town." He moved over to the door and picked up one of the boxes he had brought back from

Otis and Helen's and handed it to her.

"What's this?" she asked, taking a large box from him.

"Open it. Wait, let me get my knife. Helen taped it up so it wouldn't spill out." He dug into his pocket and pulled out a small pocketknife. When he had the tape split open, she pulled the lid open and gasped, laughing delightfully. Inside were two plain canvases, paints, brushes, art pads, and a black leather zipper case with charcoal and colored pencils tucked neatly in it.

"Where did you get this?" she exclaimed, forgetting her sadness when she saw the contents.

"One of Uncle Ralph's friends who stayed here was an artist, or at least thought he was, left all this behind when he left for parts unknown."

"So, it's all right for me to use this? What if he comes back to collect it?"

Roman laughed out loud. "We called him Roaming Roland. The last I heard he was in Peru, and that was over a year ago. I don't think he's coming back for the paints. Have fun with it."

"Thank you. I love it."

"I thought I might take one of the snowmobiles and visit my friend Jon Light Heels over at the reservation. He wants to go elk hunting." She nodded, feeling a bit anxious about him leaving. He started up the steps, then paused and called her name. "By the way, I also tried to call Uncle Ralph earlier to see if there was any news about Nick, but I couldn't get through that time either. I'll try again later. Will you be okay?"

"Yeah, I'll be okay. But will you be okay in this weather?" She didn't want to be left alone, but she didn't want to say it to him. She certainly couldn't expect him to stay with her all the time.

"The snowmobile will go where other vehicles can't. Are you sure you'll be okay? I can stay if you want me to."

"I'll be fine. Honestly. Will you be back tonight?"

"Probably."

When he left, she made sure the door was securely locked. She took out the sketch pads and began to draw. After an hour, she laid the sketch book down and smiled. It had been a long time since she had enjoyed drawing. Nick had ripped her last drawing to shreds because she had drawn a picture of a little boy playing baseball with his dad. With a smug look, he had set her sketch pads on fire, along with the charcoal pencils.

Sophia had secretly cried afterward. The picture was a birthday gift for her friend Sarah. The sketch was of her son Dylan and husband Kent. Nick wouldn't even let her explain what it was for. Just berated her for drawing a picture of a man. She had wanted to scream at Nick that at least Kent was a man and not a monster, but she had wisely bit her tongue.

Setting the drawing aside, she found a book to read. She threw the jacquard throw across her legs and plumped the pillow under her head. She read until she fell into a deep, dreamless sleep.

****

Sophia opened her eyes and smelled bacon. Her mouth watered and her stomach growled as she sat up and looked around.

"Good morning, Sophia. I hope I didn't wake you," Helen called out.

"Good morning. No, you didn't. It was the bacon. Smells good." Sophia laughed, smoothing her messy hair down.

"Breakfast will be ready soon."

"Okay. I'll just run upstairs and dress," Sophia said and hurried upstairs. As she came out of the bathroom, she heard a noise like a calf bawling. She went to the window, pulled back the curtain, and smiled. Five moose were in the yard, rooting through the blanket of snow with their snouts. The younger moose were jumping around, butting their antlers together playfully. Sophia giggled and wished for her camera.

"Beautiful, aren't they?" Sophia whirled around at the sound of Roman's voice. She had been so absorbed in watching the animals that she hadn't heard him walk in. Briefly she wondered how long he had been standing there. Stepping closer, he reached out to draw back the curtain, which she had let slip from her hand.

"Yes, they are." She could feel his warm body as he stepped closer to peer out over her shoulder. His lips touched her ear as he told her which one was the alpha moose. She felt an exciting heat surge up her body and wondered what it would be like to kiss his lips and feel his arms wrapped closely around her. Would she ever know true love? She tried to push the unbidden thoughts away, thoughts that made her heart race, but his closeness made it difficult. Finally, he took his arm down and backed away.

"I didn't hear you come in last night," she said.

"No, you were sleeping so soundly that I didn't wake you."

"Thank you for the extra blanket."

"Anytime. I have to go back to the reservation. Jon and I are going hunting again. We wounded a moose, but it got dark before we could find it, and we need to track it down. I'm not sure when I'll be back. The bison herds are near the reservation, so when we find it, I'll bring you some bison meat. Oh, and the weather forecast is for more snow."

"Stay as long as you want. I'll be fine," she lied. He touched her arm and left the room. Still shaken up by his closeness, she brushed her hair and went downstairs.

Slowly descending the stairs, Sophia's stomach growled at the smell of coffee now mingling with the bacon. As she stepped off the last step, Otis came in with an armload of wood. She shivered from the cold air. Otis dropped the short logs in the wood box.

"Good morning, Sophia. How was your night?"

"Good morning. It was fine, thank you."

"Otis, you and Sophia come and eat while it's still hot," Helen called out. Following Sophia to the table, Otis chuckled.

"That woman sure is bossy," he said.

"Maybe she has to be," Sophia replied, sitting down and helping herself to the food.

"You could be right." He chuckled again.

"Where is Roman off to?" Helen asked, setting a pan of muffins on the table. "I saw him wave and go out but didn't have time to talk to him."

"He's going to the reservation to see his friend Jon. They're supposed to be going back hunting to find a wounded moose," Sophia explained between bites. She saw Helen tense up for a moment and caught the glance she threw to Otis.

"He should know better. Another storm is brewing, and besides he needs to stay away..." he muttered through a mouthful of eggs.

"Otis..." Helen cautioned, shaking her head. With a

red face, Otis downed the last of his coffee and grabbed his coat off the back of his chair and slipped it on. Sophia watched with wide eyes, wondering what Otis was about to say.

"I'm going to the shed," he announced, his hand on the doorknob.

"Otis, you know it's none of our business and Roman still has good friends at the reservation, like Jon. We had to know that he would want to visit with him," Helen explained, laying her hand on Otis's arm and looking up at him. His face softened as he leaned over and kissed her cheek.

"Yes, you're right, but you know that I'm right, too," he said.

"I know."

He patted Helen's cheek and hurried to the shed, closing the door behind him. Helen turned to Sophia. Sophia stared at her with a puzzled look on her face.

"Helen?" She hoped Helen would explain why Otis was upset and was disappointed when she didn't elaborate. Sophia guessed it wasn't any of her business anyway.

"Sophia, I'm sorry you had to see that. Finish eating, and then I have something for you."

Chapter Nine

Nick turned into the parking lot of Dale's Grille and drove around looking for a parking place, finally settling for one in the back row between a Toyota truck and a Dodge Ram. From there he had a good view of the door and could see who was entering the building.

The diner was an older building, with a large neon sign on the roof that read: Dale's Grille. Another smaller sign was displayed in the large window announcing the featured band. Tonight, the Wayward Sons were playing, whoever they were. He guessed he would find out soon enough.

Apparently, Dale's is a popular place, he thought as he watched several couples walk in. Rebecca hadn't shown up yet, but he was early, so she had a few more minutes. He hoped she wasn't late. He liked punctual. That was one thing he could give Sophia credit for. She had learned to be punctual.

Nick looked at his watch. 6:51. He would wait until seven o'clock precisely to go in. He hoped this wasn't a waste of time and that he would be able to get the information he needed about Sophia from Rebecca. He had to find her without alerting the police to where he was. Damn! She'd pay for taking that key. He smacked the steering wheel in frustration. Why did she have to grab that bag? He thought it had been the perfect hiding place.

He had taken two serious risks by jumping bail in Georgia and shooting the trooper, but he had to get that key. He hoped she didn't figure out what it was for. Things would get ugly—quickly—if she did. He didn't want to think about the consequences. Clenching his fist, he continued to watch for Rebecca.

At 6:59 he saw her walk into the Grille. She had changed from her work clothes to jeans and a pair of cowboy boots. He got out of the Altima and stretched. Time to go to work.

Inside, he saw Rebecca sitting in a booth against the back wall. Signed pictures of musicians who had passed through were framed and hanging on the walls. The band was playing on the stage in the front corner. The place was noisy, and people were eating, talking, and dancing. Good. Maybe no one would pay much attention to them. Rebecca waved at him, and he waved back as he weaved through the moving bodies toward their table.

"This is some place," he shouted at her over the noise, sitting down opposite her. When she leaned forward to hear him better, he could see that she was wearing nothing under her shirt. It would never have crossed Sophia's mind to do that, and if it had, she would have been too afraid to. Smiling, he sat back and enjoyed the view. He just might have an easier time getting information from her than he thought.

"Yes, it's great. This is my favorite place. The music's loud, the food's good, and I love to dance."

"So, you come here often?" he said shouting, but the music ended, so he lowered his voice to just above a whisper.

"Yeah, usually Friday nights so I can wind down

from the week, but occasionally I come out on a Saturday night."

"Great. What's good on the menu?"

"The catfish plate is good and so are his cheeseburgers. But Dale grills a mean steak, any way you want it."

Nick opened his mouth to answer when their server walked up to the table, pen and pad in hand. Her name tag read: Nora. He noticed she had earrings that lined around her left ear and several bracelets on her tattooed arm.

"Hey, Becky, what'll it be tonight?" Nora's soft voice belied her outer appearance.

"The cheeseburger basket with a beer. What about you, Leon?" Rebecca asked and then called out a second time. "Leon?"

Keeping his head down, pretending to look at the menu, it took Nick a moment to realize that she was talking to him. Nodding his head, he grinned and said, "I'll have what she's having." Nick made a mental note to be more alert about his name change.

"All right. Be ready in a few." She laid wrapped silverware on the table and hustled away, handing their order through an opening in the wall behind the bar to the cook.

"Well, Leon, are you from around here?"

"North Carolina. I moved here a few months ago."

"Do you work in town?"

Nick paused before he answered, being careful not to give too much information that could be easily checked out.

"I'm working for a friend right now at his garage. Nothing spectacular, but it pays the bills."

"So, no family here?"

Biting his lip to keep from snapping at her, he realized that she was only trying to make conversation, but he hated being questioned, so he turned the tables on her.

"What about you? Live here long?"

"About two years. My parents retired and moved here from Michigan a few years ago. When Mom got sick, I came down to help out, although I do have my own space upstairs."

"They're fortunate to have a daughter like you," he said, disappointed, because going to her place was definitely out, even if she agreed to stay the night with him. Before he could say anything else, Nora set their food and drinks on the table.

"Excuse me for a moment. I need to go to the ladies' room." When she walked away, he noticed her purse on the seat, a moment he had been hoping for. He slowly reached under the table for it, but without warning, she returned and grabbed it up. "Sorry. I forgot this." Smiling, she walked away.

Nick had wolfed down most of his burger before she returned, which to his surprise was actually good. When Rebecca returned, she ate hers almost as quickly, but Nick noticed that she was much more relaxed now and more talkative. Her eyes and the smell that clung to her gave away the fact that she had taken a few hits of a joint while she was gone. Things were looking more promising.

When their food was finished, Rebecca laughed and talked about her life, her loves, and some about her job, but was careful not to mention any names or details about any ongoing cases.

Bored, Nick tried to look interested. He even let her drag him onto the dance floor, which he hated, but felt necessary to help gain her trust. Finally, he paid the bill and led her to his car.

He pushed her up against the passenger door, kissing her lightly at first and then more passionately, letting his hands slip down to her lower back. She responded by wrapping her arms around his neck and her leg around his. Sliding her hand into his hair, she pulled him closer to her. He knew she was all his. Then she pushed him back, breathing hard.

"I'm staying at my friend's house. Is there anywhere we can go to be alone?" he asked, caressing her cheek.

"Not tonight. I have to be up early in the morning, and I need to go home and pack."

"Pack?"

"Two of my girlfriends and I are going to a resort spa in the mountains. We're leaving before sunup, but thank you for the dinner."

Nick tried to hide his frustration. Sleeping with her was not anything he cared about, but it was a way to get the information he needed. This was certainly an unexpected bump in the road.

"Leon, are you okay? I'm sorry. Maybe this was a bad idea. I guess I should go." She turned to leave, straightening her shirt, but he caught her arm and pulled her to him.

"Hey, I understand. I shouldn't have expected you to stay all night with me, but I really like you. Can we meet again?"

Rebecca frowned as she thought it over. Then she smiled. "Sure. If you want to. Maybe next Friday night? Same time and place?"

"Sure thing, or I could pick you up?"

"Sure." Taking a pen and piece of envelope from her purse, she wrote down her address, directions, and cell phone number. He placed the piece of paper in his wallet, and with a last kiss goodbye, she hurried to her car and drove off.

Nick sat in the Altima for some time, deciding on his next move. He had to be careful. He didn't want Danes to catch wind that he was on Sophia's trail and move her to another place. That is if he was the one who was hiding her, but his gut told him he was, and his gut feelings were seldom ever wrong.

Chapter Ten

Sophia followed Helen to the couch. She wondered what the surprise was but was disappointed that she didn't explain why Otis was upset at Roman going to see his friend. She wanted to believe that it was because of the storms, but their tone conveyed something different.

Helen pulled a brown paper package from beside the couch and handed it to Sophia. The paper rattled, but the contents felt soft. "I made this for you last night," she said. Sophia tore open the package. Tears filled her eyes as she looked up at Helen's face.

"Beautiful," Sophia gasped. She held up a light green crocheted baby's blanket with a matching hat. "I love it." Sophia wiped her eyes on her sleeve. Oh, how she wished her mom were here. "You're very talented."

"Thank you, although I should tell you that I already had the blanket made, but I did finish the hat last night." Helen laughed. "I'm glad you like it."

"I love it." Sophia rose from her seat and wrapped her arms around Helen. Sophia knew she would always cherish the gift, and she told her so, but Helen frowned.

"Sophia, I'm sorry I let your secret out. I just assumed that Roman knew, but then he left the room so abruptly that I worried most of the night. Was he terribly upset?"

"No, Helen, it's fine. He was shocked. He spilt juice

on his shirt and went to change."

"Well, still…"

"I'll be honest with you. I didn't want Nick to find out about the baby, so I never told anyone I was pregnant, not even Mr. Danes. I thought since the divorce was over, I would never have to see Nick again. He would only want to use the child as a pawn to get what he wanted. So don't worry. It'll be okay."

"What a terrible ordeal you must have gone through with that horrid man."

Sophia sat back down, and Helen took her hands. Sophia wanted to confide in Helen, just let everything spill out, but it was too soon. Most of her past was still too painful to talk about.

"Everything *will* be okay."

"I hope so, Sophia, for your and the baby's sake. Listen, I want to tell you some—" Helen began, but her words were cut off when Otis came back in stomping snow off his boots.

"Helen, we need to finish up and leave. The second storm is almost here."

"Okay, dear." She hurried to the kitchen, but Sophia followed her. Once again, she was disappointed that Helen didn't get to finish what she had been about to say. When Otis had the wood box full, Sophia urged them to leave.

"But I have some work to finish," Helen argued.

"I have nothing but time on my hands. I can finish it. Who knows what I might find to do. I might even make a cake. I want you to get home safely."

"Maybe we should stay with you?"

"Helen, you are so kind, but I am a big girl. Now go before Otis drives away without you."

"We'll be back," Helen yelled and waved as they drove off. A heavy feeling of loneliness fell over her as she watched them leave. She began clearing the table to take her mind off the bleaker things. When the work was done, she decided to make good on her cake idea, and an hour later she had a chocolate cake with chocolate icing on the table. "Not bad," she said, stepping back to look at her creation, which had just a bit of a cave-in in the middle.

She felt nervous to have the cabin to herself. Snow falling from the roof or a tree limb grazing the side of the cabin made her jump, but she was getting used to it. Not sure what to do with herself, she moved to the bookshelf and read over the titles, surprised at the selection for a hunting cabin—*Gone with the Wind*, *To Kill a Mockingbird*, a Hemingway. There were several by authors who were unknown to her. Moving on, she found her favorites—suspense and mystery. Agatha Christie, Sherlock Holmes, Alfred Hitchcock and several Nero Wolfes. Picking an Agatha Christie, she settled down on the couch with a bottled water and a piece of cake and began to read, but not before she heard the howling of the wind and knew the storm had arrived. Thinking of Helen and Otis, she whispered a prayer they were safely home.

She read until the dim light outside turned dark, then she put away her book and fell asleep on the couch.

****

The next morning, she stretched and got up to look out of the window. A deep snow had fallen. She wondered if Roman was okay. She glanced over at his room. The door was open, so she knew he wasn't here. Feeling a bit nauseated, she ate a light breakfast and dressed. Feeling better after eating, she made herself busy with housework and laundry. With a basket of clean laundry in her hands, she entered Roman's room to lay a pair of jeans on his bed. Instead of hurrying back out, she paused to look around.

His room was much like hers, except for the manlier black and red checkered quilt with matching curtains. A comb, along with his cologne and aftershave, were neatly placed on the dresser. A picture in a tarnished, eight by ten silver frame was placed next to the mirror. She stepped closer. A beautiful woman with blonde hair was holding the hand of a dark-haired boy. Possibly Roman and his mother. Another, smaller picture was perched behind the large one. Picking it up, she recognized Roman with his arm around an exquisitely beautiful Indian woman, and they were both wearing wedding rings. Sophia felt a momentary stab of jealousy. Knowing she was snooping where she didn't belong, she returned the picture to its place and made a hasty retreat to her room.

So, Roman had his own secrets, she thought, wondering who the woman was. Could she possibly be Jon Light Heels' relative, possibly his sister? Sophia hadn't met Jon so she wouldn't know. She also wondered if it had anything to do with what happened yesterday morning when Otis and Helen had words about his going to the reservation. It wasn't any of her business, she knew, and soon Nick would be back in jail, and she would be home again in Spring City. Alone. She almost wished… Well, it didn't matter what she wished.

Chapter Eleven

Nick spent the week following his date laying low at the lake cabin. Casey was sullen and avoided conversations when he could. Nick knew he wanted to break into the office and look for the information they needed and get on with it, but Nick felt they needed to be cautious. It wasn't his body that would get thrown in a jail cell for the long haul if they were caught. Casey would certainly get time, but not like he would, especially now that he had shot that trooper.

Danes was an intelligent man, Nick would give him that, and anything that raised his hackles could prove fatal for both of them. Casey would have to be patient or else Nick would have to take care of him. Simple. Besides, he thought his plan would work well, with no one being the wiser until he found Sophia and the key.

Nick looked up when he heard a truck come down the trail. Casey was back from town with the list of things they needed.

"Any trouble?" Nick asked, getting up from the log, where he sat next to the lake. Even though the wind was sharp, he enjoyed sitting there watching the water and listening to the wind shake what few leaves there were left from the trees.

"No," Casey said, getting out. He reached into the bed of the truck and picked up a couple of bags. When he started into the shack, Nick called out to him.

"Hey, Case, hold on." Nick grabbed a box from the back of the truck and caught up with him. "Let's talk. Why are you being impatient? We talked about all this before we began."

"You want the truth? I'll give it to you." Casey spun around and faced Nick. His face was red, and he looked at Nick through narrowed eyes. Nick set the box on the makeshift table and readied himself for Casey's outburst. He could see it coming. "My gut tells me that we need to move quickly. What're you going to do when Rebecca figures you out and goes to Danes? You're playing with fire, and I don't want to get burned."

Nick strode over to the door and sat down on the broken step, chewing on his lower lip. He replayed what he could of his time with Rebecca, making sure he hadn't slipped up in his conversation.

He heard Casey walk up behind him. He turned and saw him leaning against the doorframe, arms crossed. He was staring at the lake.

"Casey, I've always trusted your gut instincts, but I believe it would be useless to break in. We're not going to find a map with a pin in the location where Sophia is. Besides, Danes probably expects us to break in. On our next date, I'll move things along quicker, if I can. As you say, Rebecca's not a dumb chick."

"Whatever you say." Casey started back into the shack.

"Casey, this will work. We will get the key back," Nick called out, but Casey had already opened the cooler and was digging himself out a drink. Shaking his head, Nick took off down the bank of the lake. He needed to think about the next step of his plan.

****

Casey pushed the door closed, popped open the tab, and sat down on his cot. Nick had taken off walking down the lake bank. Nick was angry at him, sure, but why didn't he listen? He had a bad feeling, and Nick callously brushed it off. Someone would most likely die.

Gulping the last of the beer, he lay down. Whatever happened, he would be ready.

Chapter Twelve

For the next three days, Sophia watched the snow fall. Alone. Helen and Otis hadn't been out to the cabin, and there was no word from Roman. She couldn't keep herself from praying for his safety. A couple of times she had tried her phone, always getting the same results—no service. She filled the time with painting and reading. She slept on the couch, drawing comfort from the fire.

Rising later than usual on the fourth morning, Sophia ate a light breakfast, drank the last of the juice, and cleaned up. To keep herself busy, she took out the paints and continued to work on her painting, immersing herself in the work. When she finally stepped back from the canvas, she noticed the snow had stopped and the sun was shining. She wondered about Roman. Was he okay? She missed him and wished he would come back.

Surprised, she shook her head, trying to tell herself she was only thinking about…what?

Why had she thought that? For safety reasons? Maybe. But whose safety? Hers? Roman's? He was safe at the reservation, but did she dare let herself think about being safe with him? In his arms? Sophia, you know it will never be, she admonished herself. The hope she felt earlier vaporized.

Pushing the thoughts aside, she lifted the blue parka off the hook and slipped into it, putting on the gloves that were in the pockets. She had been cooped up way too long and wanted fresh air.

Sophia pulled the door closed behind her and went down the steps into the fluffy snow. Although she was shivering, she threw her head back, loving the feel of the sunshine on her face and delighting in the dragon's breath her exhales made in the cold air. She walked around, taking in the area around the cabin.

It had been dark when they arrived that first night, and she hadn't really been out since, only seeing what she could from the windows. She was in love with the place. In front of the cabin, across the narrow drive, was the long shed where the snowmobile and ATV were kept. Trees were scattered around the shed and the other three sides of the cabin, mostly barren of leaves, except for a few evergreens that gave the landscape color against the fallen snow.

The field behind the cabin stretched out for half a mile, leading to the lake and the foot of the mountain range that surrounded the area. She briefly thought about walking to the lake, but she was already cold, and her feet were getting numb. Another time she would make the trip.

She stepped back onto the porch and grabbed a few sticks of wood to take in. Setting the key on the mantel, she dropped the wood into the box and went back for more, making two more trips. On the third trip, she pulled the door shut, realizing she was letting out heat. Grabbing up three logs, she pushed the door with her foot, but it wouldn't open. She dropped the logs and turned the knob. It would turn, but the door wouldn't open. She had pulled the door too hard, and the latch had fallen across the door. Roman had warned her that might happen. Fighting panic, she wondered how she would get in. She remembered the kitchen door. Hurrying to the door she found it too was locked. She felt in her pockets for the key. Crap, she thought, it's on the mantel.

She returned to the front door and found a thin piece of wood and tried to pry the latch up from the gap in the door frame, but it didn't work. The latch was too heavy, and the piece of wood split. She shoved against the door with her shoulder, then decided she might have to break out the kitchen window. She would do that and reach in and unlock the door.

Her face was growing numb, and she was about to step off the porch when she heard limbs cracking. Searching around the trees, she saw nothing, but heard more limbs snapping. Silently she backed up to the wood pile and squatted behind it, peering over the top log. Someone was coming through the trees next to the shed. Scared, her heart thumping, she watched the corner of the shed. Soon enough, something dark came into view. A shaggy black wolf.

As easily as she could, she slipped off the gloves and felt around the wood stack for a piece of log she could use as a weapon. The wolf raised its snout in the air and sniffed. Terrified, Sophia held her breath, hoping it couldn't smell her fear and would move on. She shuddered to think what would happen if it found her. A piece of log would be no protection against a wolf.

The wolf turned at the shed and walked toward the porch, its large paws leaving a trail in the snow. Then abruptly, only a few feet from the porch, it pricked its ears up and ran off in the direction of the lake.

Shaking, Sophia ran to the kitchen door and broke out a section of the glass with the log. She stuck her trembling hand through the opening and turned the lock. As she withdrew her hand, she sliced her palm on a piece of broken glass. Scared and in pain, she opened the door, then quickly shut and locked it. After bandaging her hand, she used a piece of cardboard and half a roll of packing tape she found in the laundry room to cover the hole, grimacing at the blood that had dripped down the remaining glass and door. Not much in the way of keeping someone out, but later she would see what she could find to secure the door until Otis or Roman returned. Rolling several paper towels off the roll, she cleaned up the blood as best she could, pitching the used towels into the trash.

Upstairs, she showered. The hot water felt good, and she willed herself to relax, hoping that someone returned soon. She felt better when she got out of the shower. The snow was falling again, and dusk was setting in. She bandaged her hand, ate and grabbed a book to take her mind off the afternoon. Before settling down with the book, she lifted a log from the box to throw on the fire, but as she did, she gasped. A faint shadow passed by the window, disappearing around the corner.

Stunned, Sophia stared into the last bit of light, her heart racing. Maybe it was Roman, she thought, peering harder out the window. She waited for him to let her know he was there, but when he didn't, she moved from window to window looking out.

She realized it wasn't Roman. He would have let her know he was here by now. Wondering where he was, she wished again that he were here with her. Had the shadow just been her imagination? She couldn't believe it was, but after the wolf and cutting herself, her brain was probably working overtime imagining things.

She grabbed her cell phone and tried to call Roman, but no service. She went to the kitchen and grabbed the butcher knife and laid it on the coffee table next to her. Wrapped in a blanket, she sat on the couch and stared at the fire, watching and listening. She finally decided that it must have been her imagination and began to relax as her eyes slowly closed.

****

Sometime later, the noise of the fire crackling intruded on her sleep. Opening her eyes, she realized the lamp was off, but the fire was burning brightly. She had not turned the lamp off. Jumping up, she grabbed the knife and whirled around. Her heart thumped in her chest when she saw a man on the darkened stairs.

"Sophia," Roman called, stepping toward her, but then paused and threw his hands up. "Whoa, Sophia, it's me."

Shaking, she realized she had been holding her breath. She dropped the knife on the end table and sat back down on the couch. She wanted to ask where he had been, but she knew it was none of her business. She felt Roman sit beside her and put his arm around her shoulder.

"Sophia, what's happened?"

"How long have you been here?"

"Just a few minutes."

"Did you come in the kitchen door?"

"Yeah, it's closer to the shed. I saw the window was broken. I was going to ask you what happened, but when I saw you were asleep, I decided to let it go until morning."

Sophia explained everything that had happened, her voice shaking as she told him about the wolf and how she had tried to call him. "I'll pay for the damages to the windowpane, but I didn't know what else to do."

When Roman spoke, his voice cracked. "You must have been terrified. I'm sorry that I wasn't here for you. Are you okay? Let me see your hand." When he gently removed the bandage, he winced and bounded up the stairs and came back with a first aid kit to redress the cut.

"And I saw someone outside the window over the wood box, afterward. It was only a shadow, but someone was out there."

"If there were anything out there, it was probably another animal prowling around."

"I'm sure it was a person."

"If you're thinking it's Nick, don't. There's no way he's going to find you." Roman finished with the clean bandage, missing the pained look on her face. Nick had been the first person she had thought of when she saw the shadow. She hoped that Roman didn't underestimate Nick's determination if he was searching for her. His violent outburst in the courtroom was bad enough, but the look he shot her with the curled lip and narrowed eyes, along with the red face, told her he meant every word he uttered. He had proved it before…

When her hand was neatly bandaged, Roman pulled her to her feet, giving her a quick hug. "I wish I had been here for you," he whispered, and then pulled away. "It's late. I'm going to secure the cabin, and then I'll check in on you later."

Sophia nodded and climbed the stairs to her room. She lay down and fell back into a deep sleep, knowing she was safe with Roman there.

****

After Sophia went to her room, Roman sat down on

the couch, his head in his hands, shaken. He hadn't warned her of the wolves that roam the area. He had been callous to leave her alone for so long. What if she had been hurt, or worse, killed by the wolf?

And what about the shadow she had seen? Could it have been Nick? He didn't think so. Uncle Ralph would have gotten him word if Nick were anywhere around here. That is—if he knew. He couldn't believe that Nick had evaded the police this long. Was Sophia right? Had they underestimated Nick? Roman checked the damaged window and shoved a chair under the doorknob. He would fix it tomorrow. When he had secured the rest of the cabin, he went up to lie down. He knew what he would do.

Chapter Thirteen

When Sophia awoke, the sun was just peeking over the mountain. She slipped into her robe and went down to the kitchen. She had bacon frying and the coffee brewing when she heard Roman coming down the stairs.

He stepped into the kitchen, his hair a black mess. He was bare chested, wearing only jeans. "Hey, breakfast smells good." Reaching into the cupboard next to her, he grabbed a cup and filled it with coffee.

"Helen and Otis aren't here, so I made breakfast. It's not much, only pancakes and bacon, but I hope it's okay."

"I'm sorry. I should have told you, but with the terrible events of yesterday, I wanted to wait. Otis has a touch of the flu. They are staying in. They don't want you to catch it. When I found out he was sick, I came straight back here."

"Maybe I should go out and help Helen. She's been so good to me."

"Otis is in good hands with Helen, and I told them not to worry about us, just to get better soon." He stood beside her to grab the plate of bacon, and her pulse quickened at his closeness. When he hugged her last night, she hadn't wanted him to let go, disappointed that he had.

He sat down with his arm hooked over the chair and

his legs stretched out, telling her about previous hunting trips, his uncle and aunt, and the cast of characters who had been guests at the cabin. She laughed at his antidotes and was pleased when he ate two plates of food.

Finished, he pushed his plate back and deeply gazed at her. Blushing, she rose and cleared the table. Her pulse quickened when she felt his warm breath on her ear as he drew near and whispered that he would keep her safe.

"I'm going to shower." He abruptly turned away and went upstairs. She had finished cleaning the kitchen when he came back down. In his hands were a pistol and a box of shells.

"What's with the gun?" Sophia eyed the weapon with a grimace. Nick had owned a pistol and enjoyed waving it around when he felt she needed to be reminded of something, and Casey always carried one in the waistband of his jeans, along with his switchblade.

"Do you know how to shoot a pistol?"

"No, well, I, um, I've shot one before, but it's been years." Remembering the time her dad took her to a shooting range when she was fourteen. It had been a disaster. She couldn't load the gun, and had missed the entire target. "I'm uncomfortable around guns." Roman looked at her almost as if he knew the reason why.

"I thought we might go out to the lake and do some target practice, that is, if you are okay with that?"

"Yeah, I think it would be fine. When do you want to go?"

"As soon as you are ready."

Sophia hurried to her room and dressed warmly. Then she bounded down the stairs, spying a down-filled coat on Roman's arm.

"Here, you will need these, since your other coat is

bloodstained." He offered her the coat with a pair of leather gloves and earmuffs.

"Thank you."

"I'll get the snowmobile while you put these on." She saw him pat his pocket to make sure he had the key as he left the cabin and headed toward the shed. She was ready and standing on the porch when she heard the snowmobile roar to life. He pulled up next to the porch. Sliding on behind him, she wrapped her arms securely around his waist.

"Hang on!"

The snowmobile glided easily over the snow, and her long hair flapped behind her. The wind was cold, but the gloomy clouds were gone. The sun shone brightly in the blue sky and felt good on her face. The ride to the lake took only about ten minutes. Exhilarated, she felt happier than she had felt in a long time.

"Wow," she exclaimed as she got off the snowmobile at the edge of the lake. "That was wonderful." She inhaled the clean, crisp air and smiled up at Roman. He took her gloved hand and led her onto the pier, kicking snow off the sides to make a path for her.

"Look." When they stood at the end of the pier, he pointed to the snow-capped mountains.

"Gorgeous! I could stay here forever," she replied breathlessly, awed by the beauty of the majestic mountains that rose toward the heavens on the opposite side of the lake. Before she could say anything further, he twirled her to her left and pointed again to a small herd of moose rooting through the snow for grass.

As she turned back around, she heard a honk, and two Canadian geese floated side by side into view.

"They're beautiful," she cried out.

"Do you know that Canadian geese mate for life," Roman explained. "And if they lose a partner, they never mate again."

"No, I didn't know that. Not like people."

Roman stared at her for a moment, making her feel that she had perhaps said something wrong.

"Your eyes match the blue in the sky," he said, his voice raspy as he reached out and touched her cheek.

She glanced down, suddenly feeling shy. Her cheek tingled from his touch. "Thank you."

"Ready to shoot targets?" He turned and led her back to the snowmobile and drove around the lake to a target area he already had set up. She slid off while he retrieved the pistol from the compartment under the seat. She smiled lightly at the homemade wooden target of a man with a brightly painted red heart already nailed to a tree.

"Like my target, uh?" he asked coming around to her. "Made it myself."

"Looks almost real."

Sophia watched as he marked off thirty yards and dug a line out in the snow with the heel of his boot. He took the shells from his pocket and loaded the pistol. She stepped behind him when he fired three shots. Following him to the target, he pointed where the bullets pierced the heart all three times.

"Good shot!" she exclaimed.

"Your turn." He returned to the mark with her in tow. Handing her the pistol, he showed her how to aim and use the sight. Shaking slightly, she raised the gun, aimed, and pulled the trigger. She felt the vibration bolt up her arm and sting the cut on her hand.

"I think I missed," she said, handing the gun back to him, but he shook his head.

"No, try again. You need to learn to use a gun." His voice was raspy again.

Sophia stood on the mark and aimed but missed a second time. Sighing, she turned to Roman with a frown.

"Here, I'll help you." He stepped behind her, holding her hands in his. She took a deep breath and tried to concentrate on what he was saying. "Hold the pistol up and look through this bead at where you want to shoot." He tapped the tiny bead on the barrel. She nodded, moving the bead to the target. "Now gently squeeze the trigger."

She pulled the trigger, and a piece of the target flew into the air. "I hit it!" she laughed, turning to look at Roman.

"You did. Looks like you blew his shoulder off." He laughed loudly. "Try a few more."

She shot a few more rounds until she hit the target in the lower chest area. Excited, she handed the pistol to Roman. He tucked it into his pocket, and as they moved toward the target, Sophia lost her footing and slipped. Roman caught her, and in one swift motion pulled her close to him, his arms tightly around her waist. She inhaled deeply, her heart thumping rapidly in her chest. He didn't release her but gazed steadily into her eyes.

"You're beautiful," he whispered. Leaning down he kissed her softly on the lips. When she wrapped her arms around his neck and responded, he kissed her more passionately, his warm mouth moving slowly down to her neck. She moaned softly, not wanting him to stop.

"You must be freezing. I need to get you back to the cabin," he said, kissing her ear.

"No, I'm not cold."

A roar filled the air. Looking around, Sophia tensed when she saw a snowmobile headed their way. Roman reached for the pistol, loaded it, and slipped it into his pocket, then gently pulled her close to him as the snowmobile approached. Roman stiffened when a man stopped beside them.

"Roman." The man nodded his head but stayed on the snowmobile.

"Jasper. What's up?"

"Who's this beauty?" Jasper asked, staring at Sophia.

So, this tall, lanky man was Hill's brother. He looked like Hill, except for his eyes and his hair, which was longer and a shade lighter, she thought as she moved from Roman's side to behind him.

"This is Sophia. Are you out for a ride or were you looking for me?" Again, Sophia noticed the edge in Roman's voice, and Jasper must have too because he turned away from Sophia and quickly explained his appearance to Roman.

"I was near Otis's when Helen flagged me down. Asked me if I saw you to send you to them."

"Thanks for the message," Roman said. There was a tense silence between the two men until Jasper started his snowmobile and drove away.

Roman put the pistol under the seat and drove back to the cabin, dropping her off at the porch with the key. Once she was inside, he drove the snowmobile across the field toward Otis and Helen's.

Sophia had wanted to go, but Roman explained he didn't want her exposed to the flu. She worried and watched anxiously for his return, praying that they were okay. As evening approached, she hoped that Roman returned soon.

Supper was on the table when she heard the snowmobile drive up. Hearing Roman stomping snow from his boots on the porch, she hurried to the door and swung it open, the cold air swooshing in and fanning the flames in the fireplace.

Roman knelt in front of the fire. When he was warm, he sat on the stool and removed his boots. She sat on the arm of the couch expectantly.

"Roman, are Helen and Otis okay?" she asked impatiently.

"Yeah. Otis is getting better, but Helen's not feeling well. She wanted me to fill their wood box and help her with a few things in the house. Dr. Rader had been there to check on them and bring medicine."

"Good. I was worried. Let me know if I can help."

"I did tell Otis not to come out here until they were both well, to get better soon, and that you missed them," he told her, getting up to set his boots on the brown braided rug under the coat rack. Never in her life had she felt as safe as she did now.

"I have supper ready," she whispered.

"Thank you," he said, but instead of heading to the kitchen, he squatted in front of the fire again. She watched him silently, wondering if something was wrong.

****

Roman could feel Sophia's gaze on him. His feelings felt like the flames he was staring at. Erratic. Twisted. Memories of the past flooded his senses and seemed to forbid him to move forward. He had tried before. He could still feel Sophia's soft lips from earlier and yearned to feel them again, but something was holding him back, telling him to move slowly. He needed time to work through his feelings…

Chapter Fourteen

Nick woke early. He watched as the warm air from the heating unit blew the brown curtains in the air, a smug smile on his face. Rebecca was still sleeping on her side, her hair falling across her face. The sheet was down around her hips, exposing freckles on her back along with a black mole on her shoulder. He grimaced and looked the other way.

Last night's date had mimicked the last couple of weeks—eating out, a dance or a movie, and then ending up here. He had begun to feel that he wasn't making much headway with her since she shut down when work was mentioned, but tonight she had been more relaxed and talkative, especially since he had brought along a bottle of champagne, courtesy of Casey.

Nick kept her glass full but drank very little himself. Soon she loosened up. With the champagne, combined with a couple joints he had brought along for good measure, she became giggly and glassy-eyed, and her speech slurred occasionally.

Cautiously, he asked a few general questions about work. Rebecca stopped giggling and stared at him, seeming to decide if she should answer or not. With an overpowering urge to shake her and demand she talk, he controlled himself and changed the subject. She had mentioned once that her bosses were outdoor sportsmen, so he thought he would try a different approach. He poured her a couple more glasses of the champagne and casually mentioned that he liked to hunt. Giggling, she told him about the hunting cabin the firm owned.

But disappointingly, all she would tell him was that the firm owned it and it was used as a place to vacation, hunt and fish or entertain clients or friends. He tried to get the location, but she either wouldn't or couldn't tell him.

"So, you've never been to the cabin?" He twirled her hair in his fingers, kissing her ear.

"Oh, no. Only the attorneys and their wives go. Once or twice a discretionary friend. The exact location is a big secret, but I do know it's near an Indian reservation." She abruptly, put her finger to her lips and giggled again. Thinking she might disclose more information about its location, he leaned closer to her.

"I can keep secrets," he whispered and kissed her lightly, tasting the champagne on her lips.

"It's also used to keep clients in protective custody," she giggled, caressing his back and arm.

"Really. Like criminals or people in danger?"

"Never criminals. People they think might be in some kind of danger." She kissed his neck.

"I bet that's rare though."

"Yeah. Doesn't happen often, only a couple of times since I've been there, but there's a nice young woman there now. Her brute of an ex-husband threatened her in court and then jumped bail and shot a trooper." Nick's heart thumped and his body stiffened. Careful, he told himself. Remain calm. He sat up for more champagne and quickly turned the conversation around so as not to appear to be too interested.

85

"As pretty as you are, I would have thought some young lawyer would have already whisked you away for a long weekend at the cabin." She pushed the glass away and instead reached for the joint.

"Are you kidding? Those old geezers. Don't get me wrong, the Danes and the Simons are great people to work for, but there's only one that's handsome enough to get my attention, and that's Roman, but I don't think I'm his type." She rolled her eyes and blew out smoke. "I've tried."

"What's his type?"

"I don't know, really. He keeps his private life out of the office."

"Some people like their privacy." He hoped more information was coming.

"Hey, do you like to hunt? Maybe we could go sometime." Nick thought she was trying to change the subject.

"To the cabin?" She sounded incredulous.

"No, but there are more places to go besides the cabin."

"Where would you want to go? What do you hunt?"

"Deer. I like to hunt deer."

"They hunt elk, moose, and bison."

"Who?"

"The lawyers." She giggled and took another hit of the joint.

"Maybe one day we can go to Canada to hunt elk, too." Nick lay back on the bed, his head resting on the too soft pillow.

"They don't go to Canada. They go to Montana."

"I see," Nick muttered and then watched as her eyes widened.

"Oh gosh, I'm so sorry. Here I am talking about work and another man."

"No problem, sweetheart, but I believe he's lost a golden opportunity to be with you. You know the old saying, one man's junk is another man's treasure." Nick realized that the saying was not quite appropriate for this particular situation, but it was all he could think of, and it made her smile and pucker her lips for another kiss that turned into a long smothering one when she entwined her fingers in his hair and drew him to her. Afterward, she had fallen asleep in his arms.

Getting up carefully, he went over to the table next to the window, glad she had left her purse out. Then he hurried into the bathroom, making sure she was still sleeping before he shut the door. She was snoring softly when he returned to the bed, but sleep eluded him as he waited for morning.

At seven, he went to shower. When he emerged from the bathroom, a towel around his waist, he saw her lying on her back, awake.

"Good morning. What time is it?" she asked, rubbing her eyes.

"Uh, seven-thirty." He lay down beside her, caressing her cheek. "Why are you looking at me with a frown?"

"You seemed quite interested in the cabin last night." She licked her lips while she gently raked her red nails down his arm. Nick tensed up, wondering what she was getting at, amazed that she could still remember. Did she suspect something?

"Not really." He willed himself to relax. "You were in a talkative mood, so I just listened, making a comment occasionally. I like hearing you talk," he lied.

"Oh." She shrugged and raised up on her elbow so that she looked down at him. "Working for an attorney makes you wary. Not everyone is honest. So, I just wondered about your interest."

"First of all, you mentioned the cabin to begin with, but it was interesting. I like to hunt, so that was the interest for me." Apparently, her suspicious nature had reared its head now that the pot, alcohol, and the heat of the night were pretty much worn off.

"Please, Leon, don't tell anyone I told you all of that." She sat up on the side of the bed and dropped her head in her hands. "I could lose my job if they found out."

"No worries, babe. I know how to keep a secret, but you never revealed its location."

"I really don't know where it's at. I just call to make the airline reservations. After that, zilch."

"Like I said, you don't have to worry. Your secret is safe." Nick smiled, knowing he almost had all the pieces to the puzzle he needed. He was on his way to finding Sophia and his key.

"Thank you." She chewed on her fingernail nervously. Nick pulled her to him, but she pushed away and went into the bathroom. Nick had to convince Rebecca her secret was safe and relieve her guilty feelings. One word from her to Danes about their conversation, and Danes would most certainly put two and two together. Sophia would be moved again, and he would be behind bars.

"Hey, how about breakfast?" Nick called out as he dressed and packed his things.

"Sure," Rebecca replied. She emerged from the bathroom a while later, her hair still wet from the shower.

"And speaking of the office, come by one day next week and let me introduce you to my coworker, Janie. I told her—"

"You told your coworker about me?" Nick whirled toward her, irritated. But of course she did. All women do.

"Is our relationship a secret?" She suddenly became defensive and she paused combing her hair.

"No…no. Of course not. I'm just, uh, surprised, and flattered, that you told people about me. I wasn't sure that you wanted people to know," he said, smiling. "Is she the only one you've told?"

"Noooo…I've told a couple of the girls in accounting."

"Well, you certainly couldn't have told them very much since I'm a simple man." He hadn't told her much about himself at all, at least not anything that was the truth.

"It's true that I don't know a whole lot about you, but you do talk in your sleep," she said, raising an eyebrow at him. "I woke up to use the bathroom and you were doing it." Nick bit his lip and wondered what he had said. Had he given anything away?

Making light of the situation, he grinned. "I had no idea that I talked in my sleep. What did I say?"

"Mostly words that were incoherent, although you did mention a key and something about a woman."

"That's crazy. I don't even remember dreaming last night."

"You sounded upset in the dream. Leon, is there something you need to tell me?" She sounded suspicious again.

"What? It was just a dream," he snapped but quickly

apologized when she stepped away from him.

"Are you married? Is that why you don't talk about yourself?" She stared at him, her face taut.

Nick felt mildly relieved. So that was it. "No, sweetheart, I'm not. I lived with a woman for about six years. Her name was, uh, Sonya, but things didn't work out and she left. As for not telling you about myself, this is it—the only interesting thing in my life is you."

Rebecca turned to the bed to repack her overnight case. Nick moved behind her and wrapped her in his arms.

"I'm sorry I snapped at you. It just caught me off guard, and you are the only woman in my life. I promise."

"It's okay, Leon, really. Let's get going. I'm hungry and want breakfast. Afterward, I need to go check on my parents."

"Good as done." He kissed her cheek and they left.

****

After a quick breakfast, during which Nick noticed that Rebecca was not as talkative as she usually was, he dropped her off at her house with another reassurance that her secret was safe with him, but she only smiled weakly at his words.

"I'll call you," he shouted as she walked away. When she went inside, he sped away to the lake house wondering if her guilt would spur her to confess to Danes. He hoped not, since he now needed only a little bit more information to find Sophia.

Dust blew around the car as he pulled up to the lake house and parked. Inside he found Casey asleep on the cot, snoring, his arm hanging off the edge. His fingers dangled over an overturned beer can. Aggravated at how much Casey was drinking, Nick kicked the cot hard enough to send Casey rolling off it.

"Get up. We've got work to do. Change of plans."

"About time. What is it?" Casey got to his feet, dusting off his jeans. He grabbed his sneakers and sat down beside Nick.

"I found out she's in Montana," Nick said and told him everything he had found out.

"Montana's a large state with a lot of ground to cover." Casey stood and stretched his arms over his head.

"Yeah, I know, but it's a start." Nick watched as Casey dug through the cooler for another beer.

"Lay off the beers," Nick growled. "I need you clear headed." He heard Casey inhale deeply, but he put the can back.

"Too bad we can't just get another key," Casey said.

"Yeah, I know."

"Are you thinking of breaking in at Danes' office?" Casey went to stand in front of the fireplace.

"Yeah. Rebecca's getting suspicious, and I think her usefulness has come to an end." Nick rose and paced across the room. "Damn, I wish I hadn't hidden that stupid key in that duffle bag. We'd be home free by now."

"But you yourself said Sophia may not know she has it."

"True, but it doesn't change the fact that she has it."

"And to think that now she's in a remote cabin in Montana, which we may never find, because you seriously threatened her in court."

"Casey..." Nick warned, his face turning red at Casey's jab. Casey wisely changed the subject.

"So, how do you propose to find the location?"

"I have two pieces of the puzzle. The first is that she is in Montana and the second is that it's near an Indian reservation. Those are major pieces, and now it's a race against time. Every day we spend here increases my chances of getting caught."

Casey nodded in agreement. "Too bad she didn't give you more information. Do you think she'll tell old man Danes about you?"

"She's already told a coworker. I was hoping to get the location from her, but I underestimated her loyalty to the company." Nick paused, running his hand through his hair. "If she tells him about me and the talk about the cabin, I'm screwed. He'll know. But on the bright side, just for a backup plan, I got this." Nick pulled a small item wrapped in brown paper from his shirt and handed it to Casey.

Casey took the package, tore off the brown paper, and pulled out a thin bar of soap with a key impression in it. He looked it over. "I know someone who can do this. Take some time and money, though."

"Do it." Nick walked out and sat down on the porch. Casey followed, but Nick stopped him before he got into his truck. "Casey."

"Yeah?" Casey waited with his arm crooked over the open truck door.

"Have I ever talked in my sleep?"

"I've heard you mumble, but nothing major." Casey shrugged, shaking his head. Nick told him what Rebecca had said. "Do you think you said Sophia's name?"

"If I did, you know she's putting two and two together."

"Like you said, we're screwed if she does, but I can take care of her, too."

"Not right now," Nick replied, chewing on his lower lip as Casey sped away. Rubbing his temples, Nick, for the first time, felt like he was running out of time, but nothing could be done until Casey returned. Going back inside, he lay down on his cot, trying to form the next part of his plan. After a while, he grinned as a plan began to take shape, easing his anxiety.

Chapter Fifteen

"Sophia, are you okay?" Roman rapped on the bathroom door and called out. With her head over the toilet bowl, she hoped he hadn't heard the horrible sounds she made throwing up.

"Yeah, just some morning sickness."

"Can I get anything for you?"

"No. I'm good." She heard him go downstairs. She followed a few minutes later, but paused on the landing at the voices floating upward. Excited that Otis and Helen were back, she peered over the banister but realized it wasn't them. Standing in front of the fire with his hands behind his back was the tall, thin man who had ridden out to the lake to get Roman. Jasper. She descended the stairs, walking over to Roman.

"Sophia, you remember Jasper. Hill's brother." She heard the tension in Roman's voice, causing her to put her guard up, but Jasper didn't seem to notice, and if he had, he brushed it off.

"Sophia. We haven't been properly introduced."

"Hello." She extended her hand to shake his, but instead he kissed the back of it. She shuddered inwardly as he lowered his gaze to her breast and hips. She quickly stepped away.

"Yes, nice to meet you too." His smiled seemed too friendly. "You're very beautiful, if I may say so." Sophia

94

felt Roman stiffen.

"Jasper is the town's mechanic and all-around handyman, but occasionally he comes this way to fish and say hi or bring me messages."

Nodding at the men, she walked toward the kitchen. "Great. I'll start breakfast. Are you hungry, Jasper?" she asked politely, hoping he would say no.

"Jasper is on his way fishing," Roman said before Jasper could answer. He left a few minutes later, followed by Roman.

Breakfast and coffee were on the table when Roman returned. He helped himself to a stack of pancakes and a cup of coffee.

"Are they twins?" she asked, pouring a glass of apple juice.

Roman chuckled. "No. Hill is older by three years, although you're not the first to think that."

"Oh, wow. They could pass as twins."

"They have a sister between them, Rosemary, but she moved to Vermont when their parents died five years ago."

"Oh, how sad. Do they keep in touch?"

"She and Jasper didn't get along, and three years ago she packed up and left. She calls Hill now and then, but I don't think she's spoken to Jasper at all. He's the one who cut off communication with her," he explained between bites.

"You would think that losing your parents would bring you closer together."

"Maybe, but Jasper accused Rosemary of stealing their father's coin collection."

"Why would he do that?"

"When Rosemary was in her late teens and early

twenties, she developed a drug habit. But she went to rehab. Hill believes, and so do I, that although she struggled with it, she stayed clean. But Jasper didn't. He accused her of going back to her old ways and taking the coin collection before probate."

"It was never found, I take it?"

"No. Unfortunately, it wasn't. It would have helped immensely to repair their relationship if it had." Roman shook his head.

Sophia finished her food and poured a cup of coffee for herself. She wondered if Rosemary looked like Hill also. She started to ask and then changed her mind. Instead, she asked another question.

"Why did Otis, um, get upset the other day when I told them you had gone to the reservation?" She saw him frown, and his face grew red; she wished she could take the words back. "Never mind," she quickly blurted out. "You don't have to tell me."

"It's fine, Sophia," he said, smiling. "I don't care to tell…" He paused at the banging on the door. Looking relieved, Roman hurried to the door and swung it open. A tall Native American with broad shoulders and black hair stood in the doorway. "Come in and get warm," Roman said with a grin. He motioned the man to the fire.

The man nodded, and after hanging up his parka, he stepped to the fire.

"I didn't hear your snowmobile," Roman said. Sophia walked softly up behind Roman, intrigued by the large, handsome man. "Oh, Sophia, this is Jon Light Heels." She stepped out and shook his hand. It was surprisingly soft.

"Pleased to meet you."

"And pleased to finally get to meet you," Jon

replied. "You're every bit as beautiful as Roman said you are." She blushed and wondered what all Roman had told him. When she caught Roman's eye, he grinned sheepishly.

"Thank you. I have coffee and breakfast ready if you'd like some."

"Coffee would be great." The man headed toward the kitchen. Sophia followed with Roman behind her. Despite his large, muscular body, Sophia sensed a warmth and gentleness about him that made her immediately like him. She laid a place for him, set more food and coffee on the table, and turned to go back to the living room.

"Sophia, where are you going? You haven't finished your breakfast?" Roman called out to her, looking at her with a puzzled expression.

"I thought you guys would want to talk?"

"Oh, no. Come back and sit with us. It's you I really came to see," Jon exclaimed, laughing and patting the chair between him and Roman, his dark eyes shining. Timidly, Sophia slipped into the chair. Reaching for her coffee cup, she glanced warily at Roman, but he smiled at her and squeezed her hand.

Jon spoke with Sophia for a few minutes, asking questions and telling her stories about his and Roman's ice fishing trips. Sophia soon learned that Roman had once broken an ankle when he slipped and his foot went through the ice. Jon laughed loudly about the incident because he had to haul Roman back to the reservation like a sack of potatoes on his shoulders. But soon their conversation turned to how to fix the motor to Jon's boat—if it was fixable.

As the men talked, Sophia remembered that she

would never have been invited to sit at the table with Nick and his friends like this. She would have been expected to leave the room. The one time she hadn't, she had sported a black eye for several days.

Nick had been the love of her life, or so she had thought. He had been her first real love and had swept her off her feet. She met him at a concert at Stone Mountain she had taken her parents to. Nick had been sitting close to her and had struck up a conversation after the girl he had been with angrily walked away.

Sophia pretended not to notice the woman leaving and had been excited with Nick's attention. She figured she wouldn't see him again since she was heading back to Tennessee, but to her surprise, he showed up the next week where she worked with a bouquet of flowers.

"Sophia," Roman tapped her arm. "Are you okay? You were a million miles away."

"I'm fine. I was just thinking how nice this is." She smiled, raising her cup to her lips.

"Will you be okay if I ride out to the reservation with Jon? I want to take a look at the motor."

"Yeah, I'll be fine." Roman raised his eyebrows at her. "I promise." Both men donned their parkas, and then Roman filled the wood box.

"You could go with us," Roman said.

"I think I'll stay here where it's warm. I might even paint some."

"I'll be back by nightfall if nothing happens."

"Oh, Roman," Sophia called as he was going out the door. "If you can, will you check on Helen and Otis?"

"I will if I can."

"Thank you, and nice to meet you, Jon," she said as he stepped out on the porch. Roman followed him but turned back. He drew Sophia into his arms, unexpectedly kissing her until she heard the engine to Jon's snowmobile rev up.

When the men were gone, Sophia busied herself straightening the cabin and then grabbed a canvas and her paints. But as she struggled to begin, her mind returned to the picture on Roman's dresser, the picture of him and the Indian woman. Not able to resist the temptation any longer, she ascended the stairs and entered his room, moving to the dresser. To her disappointment, the picture was gone. Only the picture of him and his mother remained. She searched through a couple of drawers, but she didn't find it.

Feeling guilty for going through his things, she turned to leave when a gold object caught her attention. Picking it up and looking it over, she realized it was a button with a duck's head engraved on the rounded top. She wondered where it came from. Shrugging, she lay it back down carefully and left the room.

Back in the living room, she had lost the desire to paint. Instead, she picked up her book and lay down on the couch to read until she fell into a deep, dreamless sleep. Her growling stomach woke her up. The sun had given way to darkness and more snow. She headed to the kitchen to make a sandwich and wondered where Roman was. She looked at the time—already 5 p.m. She hoped he made it back tonight.

She ate in front of the fire and was cleaning up her dishes when she heard boots stomping on the porch. Roman, she thought, relieved that he was back. But with a quick thought of the other night, she grabbed the pistol and hurried to the door.

"Hello," a man called out and sharply rapped on the

door.

"Who's there?" Sophia asked.

"Hey, it's me, Jasper. I fell in the lake and I'm freezing." Sophia bit her lower lip while drumming a finger on the door. Finally she opened the door slowly. Jasper hurried in and went straight to the fire, holding out his cold hands to the blaze. She laid the pistol on the mantel.

"What happened?" Sophia asked, as she helped him out of his frozen coat and lay it across the hearth, noting that only his coat and his jeans from the knees down were wet.

"I slipped, but not completely in, just enough to be dangerous."

"I'll see if Roman has something you can wear." She hurried up the stairs to Roman's room. Going through the drawers once more, she found a pair of worn jeans and a shirt she thought would work.

Back downstairs, she handed the clothes to Jasper. "There's a small bathroom over—"

"I know where it is," he interrupted. He took the clothes and went into the bathroom adjacent to the kitchen. "What do you want me to do with these?" he asked when he returned, holding the wet clothes in his hand.

"I'll dry them." She took the clothes and threw them in the dryer.

She felt anxious and ill at ease with Jasper in the cabin. She paused in the kitchen and watched him where he sat, perched on the couch. He picked up the book she had left on the end table and was reading the back cover. Jasper certainly looked like Hill, although he was much more handsome. But where Hill's personality was friendly and outgoing, Jasper's was dark and closed. She would ask him to leave when his pants were dry—if Roman hadn't returned by then.

"Would you like a cup of coffee?"

"That would be great. I take mine black." He turned and stared at her. Uncomfortable, she whirled around and hurried into the kitchen, where she stayed until the coffee was done brewing. Please, God, let Roman come back soon, she prayed. When the coffee was ready, she carried a cup to him and then took a seat in the rocking chair farthest from him.

"You look like a bird ready to take flight. You're not afraid of me, are you?" Jasper sipped the hot coffee. She glanced up at the pistol on the mantel and chided herself for leaving it there. Jasper caught her glance and grinned.

"No, I'm not afraid, but I don't know you. The only reason I let you in is because you were wet and a friend of Roman's."

Jasper snorted. "Friend, maybe, but not a close one. The only reason Roman puts up with me is because of Hill."

"Oh."

"Has Roman told you anything about me?"

"No. Is there something to tell?" She thought there was from the way Roman reacted to Jasper when he was around, or his name was mentioned.

"Not really." He swirled the coffee in the cup, staring as if in deep thought. "How long have you known Roman?"

"For a while, but really our relationship is—"

"None of my business." He interrupted once again. "I was just wondering what a beautiful woman like you sees in him?" She felt her cheeks get hot, but he continued to talk.

"You know, Roman has a few secrets of his own. Has he made you aware of them?" Sophia frowned, not knowing what to say. She stared at the crackling fire, thinking of the photograph that had disappeared from his dresser. "I see from the shadow that crossed your face that he's not told you about his previous marriage."

"It's not my business." Crestfallen, she continued to stare at the fire.

"Well, he was. Aren't you curious to know who he was married to?"

"No, and I would rather hear it from him." Sophia shook her head but knew he was going to tell her anyway.

"Jon Light Heels' sister, Raven."

Sophia's heart skipped a beat, and she dropped her head, biting her quivering lip. Raven. The black-haired beauty in the picture. With a pang of jealousy, she turned away from him, but from the look on his face, she could tell that he knew he had struck a chord.

"Ohhh, you didn't know that he had been married. I didn't mean to cause you any grief, but I thought that he would have been honest with you."

Sophia rushed from the room and grabbed his dry clothes, pitching them to him. "I think you should leave now."

"Look, its dark and still snowing. I'm sure Roman won't be back tonight since he's at the reservation with Jon. If I know those two, they'll drink the night away. How about I just stay here and keep you company?"

"No. Please leave. And how do you know where Roman's at?"

Without changing clothes, Jasper ignored her

question and put his boots and dry coat on, along with his gloves. He slung his jeans across his shoulder and headed out the door.

"So long," he quipped as he stepped off the porch. "Are you sure you want me to leave?"

"Yes!" Sophia shut, locked, and latched the door. She leaned against it with her eyes closed until she heard the engine to the snowmobile whine. Sitting back down in the rocker, she cried. Was Jasper telling the truth? Why hadn't Roman told her about Raven? Was that why he kept going to the reservation, to see her?

The last question hurt, but he hadn't promised her anything. She was considering her choices of what she should do when she heard boots on the porch and another rap on the door. Roman? Unlocking the door, she swung it open expecting to see Roman, but instead it was Jasper.

"Before you slam the door in my face," he said, raising his gloved hand, "my snowmobile won't start. I don't know what's wrong with it, but it's for sure I'm not going anywhere, and there's nowhere within walking distance I can go tonight."

"Are you sure something's wrong with it? I heard it start." She eyed him cautiously.

"Positive. You heard me trying to start it, but it won't run. I can walk and get help in the morning." Her instinct was to shut the door in his face, but she didn't want him to freeze to death.

"Can't you call someone?"

"Tried to. No service. Didn't Roman tell you how rotten cell service could be out here in the wilderness?"

"All right, come on in." Sighing, she stepped back from the door. "Just don't talk to me."

"I'll be quiet as a mouse," he said sarcastically. She

walked away to head upstairs, but then paused and added. "You can sleep on the couch." She could feel his eyes on her as she ascended the stairs. She entered her room, locking the door behind her. When Roman returns, I'll tell him what Jasper said and see what happens, she thought to herself. Feeling better with a plan of action, she fell into bed but slept fitfully.

Chapter Sixteen

Nick opened his eyes. Casey was standing over him, shaking his shoulder and grinning. His thin body was between Nick and the window, casting a long shadow.

"What time is it?"

"Five thirty in the afternoon."

"Did you get it?" Nick asked, sitting up on the side of the cot, rubbing his face.

"Yep." He held up a silver key and handed it to Nick. "So, what's the plan?" Casey asked. Nick sensed the nervous excitement from Casey.

"We strike tonight."

"What about an alarm system?"

"I have the code to shut it off. Can you believe that Becky carried a tag on her keychain with the code written on it?" Nick chuckled.

"I have a weird vibe about that chick," Casey blurted out.

"Don't worry. She's not the sharpest tool in the shed. She'll never suspect."

"Maybe. What about security cameras?"

"I didn't see any when I was there, but we'll have to take precautions, just in case."

"What happens when you don't show up for your date with Becky?" Casey asked, popping the tab to a drink from the cooler.

"No problem. She's going to a concert with some of her friends," Nick explained. "I made up some excuse about a family dinner with my buddy's cousins from out of town. Are you ready?"

"As I'll ever be." Casey pulled his knife from its sheath and ran his finger along the blade. Nick smiled. Tonight, they would get answers.

Nick made sure the flashlights were working, and both men dressed in the dark clothes and hats that Casey had bought at the thrift store. Then they waited.

"It's time," Nick announced when the light began to fade. The two of them jumped in the truck. Casey spun the tires and sped away. Once in town, they grabbed some burgers. Then Nick instructed Casey to park in the pharmacy parking lot across from the law office.

"We can't stay here. This place is crawling with people," Casey said, scooching down in the seat.

"Hey, all we're doing is eating our food. No one knows any different. Besides, it's only for a few minutes."

Nick took the binoculars and scanned across the street toward the law office, making sure that no one was still working and that the cleaning crew had left. Becky had mentioned that the cleaning crew was normally done around eight o'clock. All the windows were dark, except for the lobby, where a lamp was left on all the time. The clock on the dashboard read 8:45.

"Casey, see the paint store across the street and two buildings down?" Nick pointed at the dark building. Casey nodded. "We'll walk down there, then move around to the alley and walk up to the law office." Nick opened the glove box and took out two pairs of black latex gloves. He tossed a pair to Casey, who shoved them in his back pocket. Nick did the same.

Following the path Nick had laid out, they arrived at the back of the law office without being seen and slipped their gloves on. Nick stuck the key in the lock, but it wouldn't turn.

"Damn!" Nick hissed and wheeled around to Casey. "Should have known. Front door. Stay here." Nick hurried around to the front door but stopped before rounding the corner as a car passed and flattened himself against the wall. Quickly, before more traffic drove by, he squatted in the doorway and inserted the key. As soon as the door opened, he pushed inside and scrambled to the alarm box and punched in the code. Nick could only hope that no one saw him.

"Anyone see you?" Casey asked when Nick let him in.

"Don't think so." Nick shook his head. "Let's get started."

Splitting up, they searched each room until Casey called out that he had found Danes' office. Nick, who was in the room opposite him, hurried into the neat, orderly room. Nick visualized Sophia sitting on one of the wingback chairs, nodding softly at the lawyer, fear in her eyes when she heard he was out on bond.

Casey was sitting at the cherry desk, penlight between his teeth, shuffling through the drawers and files.

"Any luck yet?"

"Not yet," Casey mumbled.

Nick walked around the room with his penlight, shining the light around and then poking through the bookshelf behind Casey. They had to be missing something…

"There's nothing here. Not one mention of a cabin, a lake, or anything. Maybe I should break into the filing cabinet. I have my tools," Casey said, sounding irritated.

"No. I don't think that will be necessary. Look what I just found." He motioned for Casey. When he was beside him, Nick pointed at a picture.

"It's just a picture of three fishermen. So what?" Casey leaned forward.

"Yeah, but look closer. One of the men is Danes. Look at the sign to the left of him."

Casey stared at the picture and broke into a large grin. "Well, well, look at what we just found." He glanced at Nick, rubbing his gloved hands together.

"Welcome to Cutbank, Montana." Nick poked the picture with a gloved finger. "Our next destination." He laughed, but suddenly whirled toward the door. Casey pulled his pistol from his jacket pocket and cocked it. Someone was in the building.

Tapping Casey on the shoulder, Nick nodded to the back of the desk. They knelt behind it, hoping that whoever was in the building would leave without discovering them. Nick cursed under his breath. Was the cleaning crew just now coming in?

A fluorescent light hummed and blinked on, lighting up the back hallway. Peeking from around the desk leg, Nick saw a woman walk by.

"Damn. It's Becky." Nick cursed again in a whisper.

"What's she doing here?"

"I don't know. She was going to a concert with her friends." Nick wondered if he had tipped her off by something he'd said, or worse, had he said something in his sleep? But whatever had happened, here she was.

"We'll have to kill her," Casey remarked.

"But not here, if we can help it," Nick replied just as the lights in the office blinked on.

"Leon?" Her familiar voice called out. "I know you're here."

With a slight nod to Casey, Nick stood up, taking note of the Colt pistol in her hand.

"Ha! I knew you were up to something."

"Look, Becky, it's not what you think." Nick moved toward her, holding his hands out to his side.

"What are you looking for?" She waved the pistol at him. He stepped around so that his back was against the bookshelf. She moved to face him.

"You wouldn't understand. How did you know I was here?" he asked, keeping her attention so that Casey could maneuver around behind her.

"My work key. Guess what I found when I got out my keys?"

"No clue. Tell me."

"Flakes of soap were in the groove of my office key." She smiled at him cunningly. "So, I figured you were up to something. I just kept watch."

"Where are the police?"

"I haven't called them yet. I wanted to make sure I had something to call in." She held the phone tightly in her hand. "Now, back to why you are here. I'm guessing you are looking for Sophia."

"What?" Nick stared at Becky.

"Don't act dumb, Leon, or should I call you Nick? Do you think I'm that stupid?" Her voice became shrill. "First you talk in your sleep about Sophia, and then I find soap on my work key. How long did you think it would take me to figure it out?"

Nick stepped around the desk and moved toward

her, his hands still up. "Becky, just take a moment and listen to me."

"No way and stay back." She waved the gun at him. "You used me. I'll be glad to see you rot in jail, not to mention I'll probably get a nice reward for this." She hit the 9-1-1 buttons, but before she could press send, Casey rushed her, surprising her with a hard shove to her back. She stumbled into the filing cabinet, crying out and flailing her hands to catch herself. The Colt and the phone flew from her hand. Nick seized the Colt while Casey struck her across her temple with the butt of his pistol, a larger Smith and Wesson, knocking her out cold.

"What now?" Casey asked.

"Take her back to the cabin."

"How are we supposed to get her to the truck?"

"You go get the truck. While you're gone, I will make sure everything is put back and the lights are off. Just hurry back."

By the time Casey was back, he had everything back in order, at least he hoped he did. They dragged Becky to the truck and shoved her into the cab. Casey sped away. Only then did Nick breathe a sigh of relief.

They rode in silence to the cabin. Nick hadn't wanted it to come to this, but her stupidity had given them no choice. His thoughts churned. All this trouble because of that key. If only Sophia hadn't taken it.

Becky moaned and her head rolled until it lay on Nick's shoulder. The truck lights flashed on the dark cabin, and Casey parked the truck in front of the old porch.

"She's coming around," Casey muttered.

"You know what to do. Just do it quickly." Nick hurried into the cabin. He heard a shot, and ten minutes later Casey walked in, wiping his hands on his jeans.

"She's fish food now."

"Make sure we clean up and leave no trace evidence behind, and then we head out to the airport," Nick called out, hoping he hadn't left any evidence behind at the office.

Chapter Seventeen

After a fretful night's sleep, Sophia sat up in the bed, glancing out the window at another overcast sky. She yearned for sunshine. On the landing, she heard dishes rattling and remembered that Jasper was downstairs. She descended the stairs, ready to throw Jasper out. She was surprised to see Roman making coffee, and there was no sign of Jasper. Scanning the coat rack, she noticed that Jasper's coat was gone.

"Roman, I'm so glad you're back. Why didn't you wake me? I would have made you breakfast," she said excitedly as she walked toward him. But when he whirled around, she hesitated and drew back, inhaling deeply at his red face and glaring stare.

"Yeah, I bet you are," he retorted sarcastically, his voice cold and harsh.

Sophia's heart thumped hard in her chest, her body trembling.

"Roman?" she whispered, but he turned his back on her, pouring a cup of coffee. "Why are you angry? Did I do something wrong?" She felt sick to her stomach.

"Don't play the innocent game with me!" he hissed, stepping toward her. She stared at him in disbelief. "I should have known better than to let myself have feelings for you. I thought you were different, but…"

"How can I defend myself if I don't know what I've

done?" She choked up trying to talk.

"I really don't want to hear any of your lies! You may have Uncle Ralph fooled, but you don't have me fooled anymore."

"Please, don't do this," she pleaded. For a moment, she saw Nick standing before her, his face twisted with rage. She reached out to Roman, but he backed away and angrily threw the cup into the sink, where it shattered into pieces. Coffee splattered everywhere. He took the steps two at a time, entered his bedroom, and slammed the door shut behind him.

Sophia, with her chin trembling, went to the sink to clean up the mess while tears flowed unbidden down her cheeks. This is unfair, she thought as she picked glass from the sink. What did I do? She scrubbed the sink, falling back into what she did when Nick had been angry with her. She cleaned.

She had the coffee cleaned up when she heard him come down the steps. Wiping her hands, she turned to face him, biting her lip. Her heart dropped when she saw his duffle bag in his hand.

"Roman," she took a deep breath and called out. "I don't know what I've done, but it's not fair to find me guilty of something and not let me defend myself."

"Do I have to say it?" His lips curled. "I came back last night as quickly as I could, worried that I had left you alone again. But I guess I needn't have worried because when I came in, Jasper was coming out of your bedroom." He snorted viciously.

"No, no. He wasn't in my room! I kept the door locked all night," Sophia cried out, shaking her head fiercely. "Roman, he wasn't."

"He shouldn't have been in the cabin. Period."

"I tried to get him to leave, but he said the snowmobile wouldn't start..." She stopped trying to explain. She knew from the look on his face he didn't believe her.

"I'm going to the reservation for a few nights, although I'll check in on you daily. You'll be okay until Otis and Helen are well enough to come back, or I can get you back to Tennessee, whichever comes first." He turned to go but paused and continued. "But I just ask that if Helen does come back before you leave, I would appreciate it if you wouldn't whine to her. She has enough to deal with right now." Huffing, he left, slamming the door shut behind him.

"Roman," she called out, but he was gone.

Wrapping her arms around her stomach, Sophia doubled over and cried. His words cut like a knife through her soul. She wanted to go home, even if it meant having to face Nick. Caressing her stomach, she lay on the couch and cried until there were no more tears to cry.

****

Roman sped away on the snowmobile headed toward the reservation, a war raging inside him. He was heartbroken, but better to find out now than later. He hoped that Nick was arrested soon so that he could get back to his life. He would ask Jon to ride into town with him and try to reach Uncle Ralph and find out how things stood. Then he would go back to the reservation. Maybe he and Sophia would be going back to Tennessee soon. He hoped so. And maybe Nick had given up on finding Sophia, or yet, maybe he never intended to look for her at all. Had Uncle Ralph misinterpreted Nick's threats in court?

Chapter Eighteen

So, this is Cutbank, Montana, Nick thought as he crossed Main Street toward Louie's Steakhouse, followed by Casey who had paid the taxi driver. His stomach growled, and he ducked his head down against the cold and flurry of snow and hurried on. The plane snacks hadn't lasted long. Inside the warm restaurant, a woman with long red hair that bounced as she walked led them to a table near the bar section. Nick draped his coat over the chair as she placed menus in front of them. An inviting fire blazed in the fireplace across the room from them, and Nick could smell the smoky aroma of the oak logs that crackled as they burned.

"Your server will be here shortly." She smiled and walked away. Casey opened the menu and studied the lists of steaks, but Nick looked over the room, observing the patrons, who were chatting, eating and drinking. He noticed several cowboys, a few hunters and fishermen, and a table of women, who were laughing hysterically. But at the far table in the corner, Nick saw a tall, broad Indian. A beautiful woman with long black hair sat next to him, and across the table sat a white man with dark hair, talking angrily while shaking his head. Nick wondered what the conversation was about but dropped his head to the menu when the Indian looked at him.

A young woman arrived, introducing herself as

Amber, and took their orders. They waited silently until their food arrived.

"Hey," Nick called to Amber. "We're in town to do some hunting and fishing. Can you suggest a place that rents cabins?"

"Sure." She grinned. "Reese's General Store down the street rents cabins. They also help obtain fishing and hunting licenses, equipment, and ammo."

"What about transportation?"

"Not sure that they rent ATVs or snowmobiles, but they can hook you up."

"Thanks," Nick said, dismissing her and digging into his steak and fries.

"Got a plan?" Casey asked between bites.

"First thing we need to do is check out the general store. We need a map and a cabin."

Casey nodded and finished his food. Nick paid the bill, flipping a five on the table for the server and headed for the door, but not before noticing the Indian and his companions were still talking.

****

A small bell tinkled when Nick pushed open the wood-framed glass door of the general store and stepped inside. A large, curved, polished counter was center stage in the room. Stuffed moose and bison heads were mounted along the walls, as well as geese and an assortment of fish. A large, stuffed black bear was mounted on a wooden base to Nick's right. A stone fireplace was to his left, sporting pictures of hunters and fishermen along the mantel.

Nick strolled over to the fireplace, searching the pictures. One in particular caught his attention. Danes was holding a large-mouth bass in front of a lake,

116

grinning broadly. A dark-headed man was beside him, but he was looking down at a smaller fish on the ground. The figure seemed familiar, but Nick couldn't place why at the moment. He was reaching for the photograph when a gray-haired man walked into the room from the back. Nick jerked his hand back and turned to the salesman.

"May I help you?" the man asked, walking behind the counter. Nick read the name tag: William Reese. His wire-rimmed glasses slid down his nose, but instead of pushing them up, he looked at Nick over the rim.

"We're looking for a place to do some hunting and fishing," Nick explained.

"You picked a good place. We've got several good little cabins to choose from," Reese replied and reached into a drawer to pull out some pamphlets.

"What lake is this?" Nick pointed to the photo he had been about to pick up. "Fishing looks good there."

"That's Crescent Lake. A lot of big fish come out of there. We do have a two-bedroom cabin to rent that's a mile away but it's easily accessible to the lake by snowmobile."

"We'll take it." Nick pulled out his wallet. "And we'll need that snowmobile."

"I'll need drivers licenses, please," Reese said. Picking up the fake cards, he read the names aloud. "Leon Martin and Cory Baker. All right. Just let me get you boys a receipt and the key to the cabin. You'll have to catch a ride to the garage for the snowmobile."

"Where's the garage?" Casey asked, sidling up beside Nick.

"Three streets down. I'll call Jasper and have him pick you up. He's the owner."

"That'll be great." Nick fished in his wallet to pay.

While Reese filled out the paperwork, Nick browsed around the store. Casey went to find the bathroom. The papers were ready, and Nick was signing his name when the bell over the door tinkled again. Nick looked up to see a dark-haired man walk in and wave at Reese as he pushed his sunglasses up on his head.

"Hey, Roman, how are you? Be with you in a minute."

"No hurry, Bill. I just need some ammo. I can get it myself."

Keeping his head down, Nick scribbled his name, then took the yellow envelope Reese offered him, and he and Casey left to wait on their ride. Nick took one last look as he went out the door and smiled. Roman. The man in the picture. Danes' nephew.

"It won't be long now, Casey." Nick shoved the envelope into his new duffle bag and then stuck his gloved hands in his coat pockets.

"I hope not," Casey groaned, his hands stuck deep in his jeans pockets. "It's too fricking cold to be up here."

"I bet that's our ride coming there." Nick nodded at the brown Ford easing down the street toward them.

The truck paused in front of them, and the driver waved. Nick and Casey jumped into the cab, glad for the warmth. Casey extended his hands toward the vents, rubbing them in the warm air.

"Hope you brought gloves," the driver said to Casey.

"I did. They're in the duffle bag."

"Well, hey, I'm Jasper."

"I'm Leon and this is Ca-Cory." Nick introduced them, remembering Casey's alias at the last minute.

"Never been here before?"

"No," Nick replied, shaking his head. "First time."

"Lots of good fishing and hunting if you're interested."

"We are," Nick said.

"Where you guys staying at?"

"A cabin about two miles from the lake."

"That's Keller's cabin. Rich ole coot. I reckon they've gone back home to Louisiana. Didn't stay as long as they normally do since Mrs. Keller wasn't feeling well. Flu season hit hard for some folks this year."

"That's too bad for them but good for us since we have a place to stay that's close to the lake," Nick said.

"For sure on that. Here we are. The rides are behind the station." Jasper pulled into the service station. "Follow me."

The shed had six stalls. All the stalls except two had snowmobiles. Jasper went to a metal box on the wall, unlocked it, and took down a key from a hook inside. He handed the key to Nick. Nick noticed the fob had a number 5 engraved on it.

"That's your ride," Jasper said, pointing to a snowmobile with black stripes. "Ever driven one before?"

"Can't say as I have," Nick answered.

"Let me give you a quick lesson, and then you boys can be off."

Nick and Casey followed the mechanic to the snowmobile, and after a ten-minute lesson, he and Casey straddled the machine. Jasper showed them the trail behind the shed that would take them to their cabin.

"Happy hunting," Jasper shouted.

Yes, indeed, Nick thought as he steered the snowmobile onto the trail with Casey holding tightly to his shoulders.

Chapter Nineteen

Not knowing when, Roman might return, Sophia kept busy. She tried to push the hurt away. She missed Helen and Otis terribly and hoped that they recovered from the flu soon, but if she left before they could come back, she would ask Roman to let her say goodbye.

Surely Roman couldn't believe that she had let Jasper into her room. Yet, he did, and he hadn't even given her a chance to explain anything. What was it he had yelled at her? That he had seen Jasper come out of her room. There was no way! Her door had been locked all night.

Roman should have known something wasn't right. What had Jasper told him? Why had Roman believed Jasper and not her? A heavy sadness engulfed her knowing that Roman didn't trust her and never would. With a pang of jealousy and bitterness, she remembered what Jasper had blurted out about Roman and Raven.

Nothing to do but go home to face whatever. For the second time in her life, she was going to run away. She just hoped that Mr. Danes wouldn't find out about her and Roman. She would take the ATV to town and get a ride to the airport. Roman had let her drive it a couple times, so she believed she could handle it. She took the picture she had been painting off the easel, wrapped it in brown paper, and wrote across the front, all the while wondering what she would tell Mr. Danes about her leaving.

"Why do I have to explain myself?" she suddenly asked out loud. "Why do I even have to return to Tennessee? I have no one, really. My aunt, but we're not that close. I can go anywhere I choose. Start over. Just me and the baby." Saying it out loud gave her a sense of what? Freedom?

Not wanting to leave without saying goodbye to Helen and Otis, she sat down and hurriedly wrote out a short letter to them. Remembering Roman's words not to burden them with her troubles, she just explained she needed to return home and was thankful for everything they had done for her and would forever be grateful for their kindness. Folding the letter, she left it tucked inside the package she just wrapped for them.

She was still in the kitchen when she heard a snowmobile churning across the yard. Was it Roman? Would he cast more accusations and hurtful words at her? She didn't want to face his anger again. She already had enough to last a lifetime. She was going home. She hurried to the window and peeked out. She was deeply disappointed to see Jasper climb off the vehicle and trudge to the door.

Suddenly she was filled with fury at him for his deceitfulness. She was tempted to open the door and claw his eyes out, but she pushed the temptation away and hid silently behind the door. She heard the sharp rap on the door but remained quiet. Enough damage had been done already.

"Hey, just wanted to let you know that you have a new neighbor. They're renting out the Keller place."

When he stepped off the porch, she scooted behind

the couch in case he looked in the window. Seeing a shadow move across the floor, she peeked from her hiding place, and sure enough, he was peering through the window. She stayed hidden until she saw his shadow move away and heard the snowmobile speed off. Rechecking the doors and windows, she hurried up to her room to pack. She emerged later with her duffle bag in hand and was ready to leave when the door opened, and a large man covered in snow stepped inside.

"Otis!" she cried out and, dropping the bag, flew down the steps to greet him. "I'm so glad to see you."

"What a great reception. Hello to you, too, young lady." He laughed, handing her a large wicker basket. She set it on the coffee table and lifted the lid, smelling the aroma of fresh baked bread.

"Where's Helen?" she asked as Otis checked out the wood box.

"At home. Although she's tons better, she's still not up to par. Doc Rader thinks she needs to stay home at least another week."

"I wish she were better. I miss her." Sophia frowned. "Otis, maybe I could come out and help her with chores and things. She's been so kind to me, and I really wouldn't mind helping out."

"No, Sophia, she would appreciate it, but she wouldn't want to take the chance on you getting sick. I felt I was taking a risk just coming over myself. This flu's been bad, but we were worried about you."

"I'm fine. No need to worry. Doc Rader came and checked on me, too," she said in a forced, happy voice, but Otis' eyes narrowed as she headed to the kitchen with the basket while he filled the wood box. After several trips, he closed the door behind him and dusted wood chips from his coat into the box.

"Where's Roman?" he asked, throwing a log on the fire.

"The reservation, I think," she answered, feeling her face blush and not sure how much to say to him. She turned away, her eyes filling with tears.

"Hmm. Argument?" he asked softly, grasping her arm until she faced him.

"Yeah, but everything's fine. And it was my fault." She glanced down, scuffing the floor with her sneaker, feeling the sting of Roman's words again.

"Well, I highly doubt that it was all your fault. Don't forget that I know Roman. He can be harsh and bull headed."

"It was a misunderstanding. I made the mistake of letting Jasper into the cabin and—"

"Say no more," Otis said, holding up his hand. "Jasper…" Otis repeated his name as if it left a bitter aftertaste on his tongue. "That snake."

"I didn't know."

"Sophia, Jasper is a real piece of work. Nothing like his brother Hill. Don't let him back in if no one is here. He lives to cause trouble. Especially for Roman."

"I won't. I promise."

"I'm leaving now. Do you need anything?" he asked, with his hand on the door. Sophia shook her head.

"One more thing before I go." He pointed a large, crooked finger up the stairs. "When I came in, I noticed you had a bag in your hand. That's one reason I thought you and Roman had an argument. If you're planning on leaving, please rethink it. Although the snow's let up for now, it's still bitterly cold." He gazed steadily at her. She blushed.

"And if you're planning on riding the ATV, again, please don't. You could, and most likely would, have an accident, since you are unaccustomed to handling one." Sophia nodded slightly. She would think about it. "And one more thing. Maybe I shouldn't say anything, but I'm going to. Think about giving Roman a chance." He gave her a quick hug and a smile and left the cabin.

Locking the door behind him, she hurried upstairs to her room. She sat on the bed, debating her options. Was it foolish to think she could just pack and leave this time? With a sigh, she realized that she had more than just her own safety to consider now. But she didn't know if she could face Roman again. He certainly hadn't given her a chance to explain what had happened. So why would Otis ask her to give Roman a chance? Did he know something she didn't? Probably. She knew very little about the secrets that had occurred here.

"Why wouldn't he just listen to me?" she shouted out, the frustration and hurt overflowing from within her. She grabbed the duffle bag and flung it angrily across the room, watching it slide into the bathroom. "I didn't do anything wrong!" Weeping uncontrollably, her pent-up emotions took over, and she fell across the bed, pounding her fists into the pillows until there were no more tears to cry.

Chapter Twenty

Nick was kneeling in front of the fireplace, placing logs on the fire when Casey rushed through the door. Standing up, he watched Casey shed his boots and coat, then miss the coat hook. His wet coat fell to the floor in a heap.

"See anything?"

"Yeah, but not much." Casey stretched his hands toward the flames. "Sophia is there all right. That man, Jasper, who rented us the snowmobile, drove out there and shouted for her to open the door, but she didn't. Then he shouted that he wanted to tell her about us."

"About us?" Nick asked. His voice turned hard while his face showed deep concern.

"Not particularly about us, but that she had neighbors now." Nick stared at Casey, his lips pressed tightly together. He wondered what that man's game was.

"What exactly did the man say?"

"He yelled through the door that he wanted to tell her about the people who had rented the Keller's cabin. The door didn't open, so he shrugged and drove away."

"So, you don't know that Sophia is actually there? She didn't come to the door."

"Not then, but I did see her."

"You saw her…" Nick remembered the last time he

had seen Sophia. She was seated in the witness chair of the near empty courtroom. She had been pale, with dark circles under her eyes, and she had lost weight. Danes was questioning her, and she was answering in a soft, meek voice, twisting a tissue in her hands. She had kept her eyes either on Danes or the judge, averting her eyes away from him. His anger rose not only from her condemning testimony but because she refused to look at him. Without warning, he had exploded. Rushing at her, spewing threats and calling her a liar until he had been thrown to the floor by guards, cuffed, and toted off to a cell. It had been an impulsive and reckless act on his part.

"Yeah." Casey nodded, taking a seat on the leather sofa in front of the bay window. "An old man drove up on a snowmobile carrying a large basket and let himself in. I left the snowmobile behind a shed, and sneaking up to the window, I saw him give the basket to Sophia, bring in wood, and then he sat down and talked with her. After a few minutes, he left."

"I bet he was the caretaker." Nick left the fire and strode over to the side window and peered out.

"Probably." Casey lay out on the sofa, folding his arms behind his head and closing his eyes.

"Tomorrow, I want you to do some more scouting," Nick stated, his back still to Casey. "Make sure who's staying at the cabin."

"Uh, Nick, what do we do if she's lost the key or just thrown it away or hid it?" Casey peeled open an eye and glanced over at Nick. Nick wheeled and glared at Casey. "Just throwing that out there as a possibility," said Casey, throwing his hands up in defense.

Without answering, Nick strode into the bedroom,

slammed the door shut behind him, and fell across the bed. The thought had already crossed his mind, but Casey saying it made it a reality. No matter what, revenge would be his. Sophia would pay for crossing him.

Chapter Twenty-One

The last rays of the sun were filtering through the bedroom curtains when Sophia opened her red, swollen eyes and licked her dry lips. Her stomach rumbled. Remembering Helen's bread, she slipped off the bed. When she opened the door, she heard a noise downstairs. Grabbing the pistol from the nightstand drawer, she tiptoed out on the landing and looked over the railing. A clattering of dishes was coming from the kitchen. Jasper! How did he get in? The words screamed in her head.

Silently she descended the stairs, but on the last step, she paused. Roman appeared holding a sandwich. His eyes fell to the pistol in her hand.

"I would rather you not shoot me," he said flatly.

"I heard a noise and didn't know what it was," Sophia replied coldly.

"Or who?"

"Or who."

Sophia strode past him and lay the gun on the kitchen table. Silently, she fixed herself a sandwich from the home-baked bread, along with a glass of tea. She took her food to the rocking chair and picked up the book she had been reading. Roman followed her and sat opposite her. She read while she ate, or at least she pretended to read. The words blurred on the page, and she could feel Roman's eyes on her, but she was determined to ignore him. She was still hurt and angry.

"So, I guess you are going to ignore me and not talk to me?"

"Should I talk to you?"

"Sophia, please I want you to listen to—"

"No!" Raw anger spewed out of her. "I'm tired of doing all the listening. I want to go home. I'm packed, and I want to be taken to the airport. I didn't do anything wrong, and you wouldn't even give me a chance to defend myself. I'm tired of being treated like I'm nothing!" She jumped to her feet, spilling the book and the food to the floor.

"Sophia, I'm trying to apologize." Roman swiftly moved to her, and before she could resist, pulled her into his arms. "I'm sorry, Sophia." He repeated it over and over, stroking her hair.

He lifted her face toward his and gazed into her eyes. Not sure how she felt, she turned her face away. Her mind told her to resist, to push him away, but when his lips found hers, her body responded to his fiery kiss.

"I know what happened, and I'm sorry I didn't believe you, but please hear me out." Taking her hand, he led her to the couch and sat beside her. "I know what Jasper did. I also know you were totally innocent. I confronted Jasper," he explained, rubbing the knuckles of his right hand.

"I don't understand why you didn't believe me."

"Again, I'm sorry. Undoubtedly, he heard me drive up and hurried up to the landing. When I came in, he had his hand on the doorknob of your room. He was only wearing boxers and his hair was all over his head. I guess I just lost it. Jasper is a liar and a cheat."

"At least you know the truth now."

"But I found out something else too. You remember the night you were alone and thought you saw someone outside?"

"Yeah."

"You did see someone. It was Jasper sneaking around."

"How do you know it was him?"

"I found this button on the ground under the window when I went to have a look around." He dug into his jeans pocket and pulled out the gold button she had seen on top of his dresser. "When I confronted Jasper this afternoon, he had a button missing from his coat. This button."

Sophia shivered, but not from the chill in the air. She wondered how many times he had been peeking in the windows, watching them, watching her. Instinctively, she caressed her growing stomach. "That's creepy."

"Yeah. He's a real snake in the grass." Sophia didn't tell Roman that was what Otis had said.

"Then why let him come around?"

"I try to be civil mostly because of Hill, and well, although Jasper's caused a lot of trouble, he did help me out of a jam." Raising her eyebrows, Sophia waited for Roman to continue. "It's time you know my secrets."

Sophia inhaled deeply, readying herself for whatever secret he was about to confide in her. A shadow momentarily crossed Roman's face. He was silent as if collecting his thoughts. She squeezed his hand, hoping he wouldn't change his mind.

"I was married to Jon's sister, Raven," he began, after taking a deep breath and raking his hand through his hair. Sophia nodded, feeling a twinge of jealousy. "Raven had been engaged to Jasper, but she suddenly broke it off with him. She never gave a reason why. After their break-up, I took her out. Jasper always blamed me for their split, although Raven told him, on several occasions, I wasn't the reason. He knew that, but didn't want to admit it."

Sophia remained silent. She could tell Roman was nervous from the way he twisted his hands together. Before he continued, he stepped to the fireplace, tapping his finger along the edge of the mantel.

"Raven and I married, against Jon's advice, and soon she became pregnant. Everything went well for the first six months." Startled, Sophia frowned. Did Roman have a child he never told her about? She opened her mouth to ask, but Roman continued. "We had been living in Tennessee so I could work, having moved there a few days after the wedding. Raven wanted to have the child at the reservation with her family. We traveled back here to stay until the baby was born, but a week after we arrived, I found her 'visiting' with Jasper. Apparently, she still had feelings for him." Sophia could see his pain.

"We fought, but finally agreed to work things out, and she promised that she and Jasper were over. We worked to move on. Three weeks later, she went into premature labor. I wanted her to go to Cutbank Hospital in town, but she wanted to go to her family."

"Oh no," Sophia said, more to herself than to Roman. She felt she knew what was coming next and again caressed her stomach.

"I didn't know what to do, so I begged her to go to town where she could get medical care, since there was a problem, finally convincing her. We took off for town. I tried to contact Jon but couldn't reach him. In town, we happened to pass Jasper walking near Louie's Restaurant. Raven called out to him and rapidly explained what was happening. She asked him to get her family. Jasper agreed to go to the reservation. Unfortunately, Raven and the baby died before her family arrived."

Roman bowed his head and took a deep, sorrowful breath. Sophia knew he was hurting. "Roman, I'm so sorry. I truly am." Sophia bowed her head, her eyes moist, sorry for his pain and his loss. "Was it placenta previa?"

"Yeah. How did you know?" His blue eyes stared into hers.

"I worked in an obstetrics office. You don't have to continue if you don't want to. I can see this is hard for you."

"No. I want to tell you." He sat back down beside her, taking her hands. "Her family was angry with me for not taking her to the reservation since she had wanted to be with them to have the baby. I tried several times to explain what happened, but they believed I was lying about what she had agreed to. It was Jasper who unwittingly told Jon why Raven had agreed to go to Cutbank, although he didn't realize at first that her family held me at fault."

"So that helped you? But why didn't Jon want you to marry Raven?"

"Yeah, Jasper cleared me. Jon had been afraid that Raven would turn back to Jasper. Her feelings for Jasper had been strong. No one knew why she left him...but I loved her, too."

"I see."

"Anyway, her family was distraught, and her mother was devastated. Although Maggie knows what happened, to this day, she still believes that if I had taken

Raven to the reservation, she and Grayson would still be alive."

"Sometimes things happen that we can't control. Is that why Otis was upset that you were going to the reservation?"

"Otis and Helen worry a lot. Mostly that I can't take care of myself in a snowstorm." He chuckled. Sophia was relieved to see some of the sadness lift off him. "But." There was a long pause. "But Jon has an older brother who still carries a slight grudge against me. He lives in Canada now but comes home periodically to hunt and visit with family. Otis had warned me previously that Henry was home."

"Oh, Roman, has he hurt you?" she asked, her eyes wide.

Again, Roman chuckled. "No. And I think the old grudge is dying. He actually asked me to go hunting with him sometime and that's a big step for him."

"I'm glad for you. You seem to be very close to Jon and his family."

His eyes searched hers for a moment. Then he stood and pulled her into his arms, holding her close. "Sophia, I have often thought about Raven and what my son would be like, but I am learning to put the past behind me. There will always be that soft spot in my heart, and I know that we've known each other only a short time, but I want you to know that I have fallen deeply in love with you."

His words caught her off guard. Her emotions whirled as he lifted her chin and once more his lips sought hers, kissing her lightly at first, then more hungrily, igniting a fire that soon engulfed her.

Chapter Twenty-Two

The next morning, Sophia awoke happier than she had been in a long time. Sunlight beamed into the room. She heard pots banging in the kitchen. Roman's fixing breakfast, she thought and hurriedly pulled on a pair of sweats, the only clothing she felt comfortable in now, combed and pulled her hair into a ponytail. The smell of bacon filled the air when she exited the bedroom and descended the stairs. That's when Helen stepped into view.

"Helen!" Sophia exclaimed, throwing her arms around the elderly woman's neck.

"I was just about to call you down for breakfast. How are you?"

"I'm good, but how are you? Are you well?"

"Getting there, I reckon." Helen moved back to the kitchen, taking biscuits from the oven.

"Helen, if you're not well, I could have fixed breakfast."

"Nonsense. I feel fine. Doc Rader doesn't always know what I know." Sophia laughed, remembering his last visit with her. He had looked at her over the rims of his glasses, which sat on the tip of his nose, and impudently told her that she needed to stay off her feet more, although she tried to tell him that she felt fine.

"Have you seen Roman?" Sophia asked, grabbing

jelly from the fridge.

"No, dear, I haven't. I thought he was still asleep…" Helen paused, looking deeply into Sophia's sparkling eyes. Blushing, Sophia turned away, setting the jelly on the table.

Sophia was saved, for the moment, from Helen's knowing glance. The door opened, and Otis came in with an armload of wood.

"Good morning, Sophia." He paused and stared at the two women. Then he winked at Sophia and dropped the wood into the half-filled wood box. Kneeling on the hearth, he carefully scraped a pile of ashes into a pail to carry out.

"Otis, did you see Roman this morning?" Helen called out, her hands on her hips.

"Sure did, but only for a moment after I dropped you off at the porch. He was in the shed getting ready to leave for the reservation. Said he was getting some fish from Jon and going to town for some supplies." Otis stood up with the pail in hand and smiled at Sophia, his eyes twinkling. "He also told me to tell you he left a note for you on the nightstand. He didn't want to wake you." For the second time that morning, she blushed.

"Thanks, Otis."

Otis went back outside, and Sophia followed Helen to the kitchen. She wanted to say something to her, but suddenly she felt shy and awkward. Not sure what to say, Sophia busied herself setting the table. She didn't know how Helen was taking the news about her and Roman, but she didn't have to wait long to find out.

"I've known for a while that Roman was falling in love with you. I could tell from the way he looked at you." Helen spoke softly, letting the fried eggs slide onto a plate. Sophia nervously picked up a paper towel and twisted it, listening closely. "Has he told you anything about himself?"

"Yes. He told me about Raven and his son."

"Roman is like a son, the son that we could never have," Helen continued. "But after what happened with Raven and Grayson, I wondered if he would ever let himself love again." The picture of Raven and Roman that had been displayed on his dresser flashed through Sophia's mind. Helen paused and washed the frying pan. She set it in the drainer and wiped away a tear that rolled down her cheek. "Sophia, I don't ever want to see Roman hurt like that again."

"I, um, I understand." Sophia frowned, feeling disheartened. Did Helen not approve?

"Of course," Helen continued, "I don't have to ask if you love him. I could see it in your bright eyes this morning." She took Sophia's hands in hers. "Roman can be gruff and stubborn, but he has a big, loving heart. I hope things go well for you two."

Love for Helen swelled in Sophia's heart, and she hugged Helen again. "I just love you!" Sophia exclaimed joyfully, wiping tears of happiness off her cheeks.

"I love you, too." Helen laughed gaily.

"Whoa there, what did I miss?" Otis called out as he stepped into the kitchen. Startled, Sophia wheeled around. She hadn't heard him come in.

"Just some girl talk," Helen explained with a chuckle and took his hand. "Better eat before it gets cold."

After they had eaten and cleaned up, Otis declared it was time for them to leave. "I have to fix the barn gate before it gets dark."

"Wait," Sophia called out before they were out the door, remembering she had a surprise for them. She grabbed the picture next to the door and handed it to Helen, remembering to remove the note she had inserted previously. It was a painting of a red and orange sunset at the lake, with moose grazing nearby.

"Sophia, it's beautiful. I adore it," Helen cried out, holding it up for Otis to see.

"Sophia, you have a great talent," Otis said, admiring the picture.

"We'll hang it over our mantel," Helen declared.

"Good idea," Otis agreed.

After another thank you, the pair left the cabin and drove away. Sophia locked the door, feeling content. For the first time in a long time, she was truly happy.

She climbed the stairs and went to her room to grab the Hitchcock book she had been reading. With book in hand, she glanced out the window and inhaled sharply. Someone was speeding across the meadow toward the lake on an ATV.

"Jasper," she growled, visualizing him creeping around again. She strode to Roman's room and took the pistol from the nightstand drawer and returned to the fireplace. "If he thinks I won't shoot him, he's got another think coming," she said to the moose head above the mantel.

****

Sophia was dreaming about her mom when she was roused from sleep by the door rattling. Sure it was Jasper, she reached for the pistol, but swiftly laid it back down when Roman stepped through the door, a gust of cold wind swirling in with him. He set down the box he was carrying next to the hearth.

"Sophia, were you afraid again?" He nodded toward the gun while taking off his coat.

"Not so much afraid as annoyed. I saw Jasper darting across the meadow toward the lake on an ATV this morning, just after Helen and Otis left. I don't want any more trouble with him."

"Helen came out with Otis? I didn't see her. I was in the shed."

"Yeah, she said she felt much better, although Doc Rader didn't agree with her."

"I'm glad she's better, but it wasn't Jasper you saw earlier, because he was in town helping Hill fix the radiator on his truck. And I had another talk with Jasper. I'm pretty sure he won't be a bother again."

"Oh. I wonder who it was."

"Probably one of the guys who rented the Kellers' cabin looking for moose. I hear they want to do some big game hunting."

"How many guys?" Sophia asked, concerned. She had thought it was Jasper because his body shape looked familiar. Could it be Casey? He was about the same height and build as Jasper.

"Don't know. A couple maybe."

"Um, Roman, have you spoken to Mr. Danes lately?"

"Not in the last three or four days, and with all that's been happening, well, I guess I haven't. Anyway, he said he would send word by the sheriff if anything came up, since phone service is so bad out here."

"Maybe we should try to call him, you know, just to touch base." She began to pace in front of the fire, twisting the hem of the sweatshirt and chewing on a fingernail.

"If Uncle Ralph had any news, he would have contacted us."

"I know," she replied, forcing herself to sit back down. Outwardly she pretended to blow it off, but inwardly her heart was racing.

"Tell you what. Tomorrow I'll go into town and try to contact Uncle Ralph."

"Thank you," she said and sighed.

"Hey, maybe you would like to ride into town with me. The roads are getting better to travel on. We can take the ATV, if it's okay for you to ride." He picked up the box and took it to the fridge. The smell of the fish made her nauseated, but it passed when he walked on with it.

"I would like that, and yes it will be fine, as long as we don't tell Doc Rader." She smiled at Roman's hearty laugh. She relaxed. Roman was right. Mr. Danes would have contacted them one way or the other if anything had happened, and there was no way Nick could have found out where she was.

Chapter Twenty-Three

Nick was frying ham when Casey swept through the cabin door, pulling his coat and gloves off. He changed into dry jeans, and then he poured a cup of coffee and sat down at the table.

"Man, its cold out there," he said and took a drink of the hot liquid.

"Forget the cold. Did you see anything this time," Nick asked as he sat down to eat. He stabbed a piece of meat with his fork and grabbed a biscuit. Casey stuck a piece of ham in a biscuit and began to eat, too.

"An old man and woman were there. The same man that was there before with the basket."

"The caretakers." Nick nodded and shoved another bite of hot ham in his mouth. "No one saw you, did they?"

"Nope." Casey shook his head but averted his eyes. Nick knew Casey well enough that this was a sign he was hiding something.

"Casey, you're lying. Were you seen?"

"No. Hell, almost. After I hid the ATV a few yards from the cabin, I snuck up to the shed. I was about to creep up to the cabin when the caretakers arrived. Then the dark-haired man walked out of the shed and talked with the caretaker. I hid until he left. Afterward, I did get a quick peek into the cabin, but only a quick one. I was cold and numb, so I left."

"When you finish eating, draw me a layout of the cabin and shed."

"Yeah, okay. But, you know, I came back by way of the lake and saw three moose grazing close to the shore. I wish I had taken the rifle. Next time I will."

"If I remember correctly, the lake is past the cabin. Are you sure you weren't seen?" His voice rising and stern as he looked up from his plate.

"Yes. And what if I was? I'd just be another hunter."

"Maybe, unless it was Sophia who saw you." Nick chewed on his biscuit and stared at his cousin.

"I'm pretty sure that no one saw me," he answered gruffly, shoving a piece of ham in his mouth and chewing loudly.

"Just pretty sure?" Nick asked, sarcastically. "What if she saw you?"

"I had on an overcoat and a hoodie. So, what if she did? As I said, I would just be another hunter. Besides, she doesn't know we're here!" Casey hissed angrily and shoved back from the table. He strode to the window and stood with his back to Nick. "Just when do you plan to make a move and get the key?"

"Soon, but I want to be prepared. I need to know the layout of the cabin so I know what to expect. I can handle Sophia. She'll cower like a puppy, but I prefer her to be alone." Nick wondered if Sophia was sleeping with that man, Roman. She was such a prude that probably not, but he didn't care. All he wanted was his key back and then what? Kill Sophia? Yeah. He wanted to wrap his hands around her slim throat and squeeze the life out of her for what she'd put him through.

"Do you have a plan?" Casey asked, his anger

almost gone.

"Yeah." Nick scooted the wooden chair back from the table and carried the dishes to the sink. "Let me lay it out for you."

Both men sat down. Nick studied the drawing Casey made of the cabin, and then explained his plan. After thirty minutes, he stood up and stretched his hands over his head. The plan was simple. Action. Swift and deadly.

"Who knows, she just might hand the duffle bag over with no problem," Casey suggested, settling down on the couch.

"Oh, she'll hand it over, one way or another."

"What if that man is there?"

"Which one?"

"Either one, but I'm thinking about the one she's probably sleeping with," Casey said, placing a large, square throw pillow under his head. Nick flinched.

"Kill him, too," Nick said coldly, staring into the fire.

Chapter Twenty-Four

"Are you okay?" Roman called out through the bathroom door after rapping on it. Sophia had to wait to pull her head from over the toilet before she could answer.

"I will be," she gasped before the next nauseous wave hit.

"Can I do anything?"

"No, it has to run its course."

When she was able, she moved to the sink and studied her reflection in the mirror, gazing at her pale lips and cheeks. She splashed water on her face and brushed her teeth. Emerging a short time later, she still felt nauseous. Roman was sitting on the side of the bed, wearing only his jeans.

"I'm afraid you'll have to go to town alone. I won't be able to make it."

"Still sick?"

"Yeah. I really wanted to go." Sophia caressed her swelling abdomen. Of all days for the morning sickness to hit. She had been looking forward to getting out of the cabin for a while.

"Is there anything I can get you in town?"

"Yeah. A Sprite would be great."

"Sprite?"

"Yeah. A Sprite and a blueberry muffin was Mom's

care package when I was sick," she explained, laughing, but suddenly she missed her mom intensely, and tears welled up in her eyes. She felt Roman's arms pull her close to him until her tears were gone and all she had left were sniffles.

"Better?"

She nodded and followed him downstairs to the kitchen. After a light breakfast of toast and coffee, he got ready for town.

"Don't forget to call Mr. Danes," she reminded him as he stepped out the door.

"My main reason for going to town, oh, and the Sprite." He kissed her and left.

After checking the doors, which was routine now, she threw logs on the fire and watched the embers fly up the chimney. She would miss the fireplace when she returned home. With a twinge, she wondered how things would change when this was over.

Sighing, she rested on the couch. Otis and Helen wouldn't be coming today because of business at the bank they needed to attend to, so she guessed she'd finish reading the last three chapters of her book while she waited for Roman to return.

****

Not long after Roman left, Sophia once more felt a wave of nausea. Dropping her book on the floor, she rushed to the bathroom. Afterward, she ate more toast and drank a little water. Beginning to feel better, she decided to paint. She moved the easel to the side of the staircase, then sat down on a stool she found in the laundry room and began painting. She wanted a picture of the cabin to take home with her. She was done painting the chimney and moose head when she heard the lock shake and the door open. Roman rushed in. It was just past noon.

"Wow that was a quick trip. I thought…" Sophia paused at the anguish on Roman's face. "What is it?" Her heart raced, and she broke out in a cold sweat.

"Come and sit down." He moved to her side when she was on the couch and took her hands in his cold ones. A million thoughts flew through her mind as her eyes searched his. Had something happened to Otis or Helen?

"I was able to get through to Uncle Ralph. He was trying to get word to us but had decided to come up here himself. I told him to wait and take care of things there."

Sophia pulled her hand from Roman's, moving it to her throat. "What's happened?"

"The office was apparently broken into over the weekend."

"Nick!" she exclaimed with a sharp intake of breath, interrupting Roman. "He *is* searching for me. He wants to kill me." She finally had to face the truth of it.

"Sophia," he paused, taking her hands back in his. "Not only was there a break-in, but Uncle Ralph's secretary, Rebecca, is missing. She didn't show up for work yesterday, and, well, the cleaning lady, Lucy, when she was cleaning last night found a bloody necklace under Uncle Ralph's desk. It has been identified as Rebecca's. An investigation is underway."

Sophia's body trembled, and dropping her head in her hands, she cried, "Oh, Roman, it's all my fault. I've put everyone's lives in danger."

"No, Sophia, you haven't. So far, no one knows what's happened, and Lindsey, the office manager, did tell Uncle Ralph that Rebecca had a new boyfriend. A man named Leon Martin. Is that name familiar to you?"

Sophia shook her head. "Do they know its Rebecca's blood?"

"DNA hasn't come back yet, but she was seen wearing the necklace at work on Friday."

"So, she could still be alive?"

"Yes. It's possible."

"But doubtful, because of the bloody necklace." Sophia's thoughts whirled. She felt responsible for all this.

Roman shook his head and pressed his lips together, giving Sophia the impression that he was holding back something.

"What now?" She wiped tears from her eyes.

Roman let go of her hands and went to stand in front of the window, staring out. "I'm not sure. Your safety is my main priority." He ran his hand through his mane of dark hair, sighing heavily. He scratched his beard and leaned against the mantel to face her. "Sophia, I know you and Nick had a stormy marriage, and I know he hurt you bad, but is there any reason he would hurt, maybe kill, someone to find you? Do you know something that he's afraid you'll tell?"

"I can assure you, I've had those very same thoughts. And no, I don't know of anything. He shared nothing with me. In the courtroom when he threatened me, I was puzzled then, too. I would have thought that he would have been glad to see me go. He said I was an embarrassment to him." Sophia saw Roman's mouth tighten.

Roman gazed at her, chewing on his lower lip. He traced his finger along the edge of the mantel. She waited, watching the fire burn down. "I think you do know something," he began, but when Sophia stood up and started to protest, he threw up his hand to quiet her. "Let me finish." She sat back down, a hurt look on her face. "I think you know something that may not seem important to you, but it is to him. It could be a conversation you overheard, something he did that seemed ordinary to you but to him critical if you ever mentioned it to anyone."

She had to admit that maybe Roman was right. Other men were over at the house frequently, but they usually talked with Nick in the garage, or she was scooted off into the bedroom to wait until they left. She told Roman this.

"Yeah, sounds suspicious to me. Illegal dealings going on. Maybe drugs."

"Do you think Nick knows where I am?" she asked anxiously. She felt ill again, and her head throbbed.

"I doubt it. Uncle Ralph has always been careful about keeping our location secret in the office, but *if* Nick did think we had you hidden away, he couldn't have gotten any information from Rebecca. None of the staff knows the exact location of the cabin. Just me, Uncle Ralph, and his partners. Even though the secretaries sometimes make the airline reservations, the airport is quite a distance from here."

Still shaking, Sophia bowed her head, visualizing the red-headed secretary who had been so nice to her. "I hope Rebecca is still alive, but if she fell into Nick's hands, I'm afraid she's dead."

"I feel the same way. Nick has already proven he's not afraid to kill anyone," Roman agreed.

As another wave of nausea hit, she sprinted to the bathroom. In a little bit, there was a rap on the door.

"Are you okay?"

"Yeah." She washed her face and then rejoined Roman on the couch.

Roman wrapped his arms around her protectively. "I love you, Sophia, and I promise not to let Nick hurt you or the baby." Never had anyone made her feel this safe or loved before.

"I just wish I knew what was driving him to search for me or even kill me." Rising from his shoulder, she gazed into his clear blue eyes. Eyes that she wanted to drown in. She felt his strong hand caress her cheek, and then he kissed her softly on her lips.

After a while, he stood up. "I'm going to gas up the snowmobile and cut some wood. The box is getting low. Sophia, try not to worry. Everything's going to be okay. I'll see to that."

"All right. I'll start fixing dinner." She stood and nodded her head, but she couldn't stop worrying about Rebecca. She knew that the probability of the secretary being alive was practically zero.

Roman spent the afternoon cutting firewood, and when he came in, she had dinner on the table. Although she hadn't turned on the lights, she was waiting for him in the glow of the crackling fire.

"Dinner smells good," Roman said, dropping an armful of short logs into the box.

"Thank you. Manicotti. My mom's recipe." She laughed lightly and stepped toward the door, closing and locking it as he dusted pieces of bark from his coat.

"You feeling better?"

"Yes, although I have to admit I'm still worried." She took his coat and hung it up.

"Like I said, everything will be okay."

"I know. Anyway, let me flip the light on so you can

eat." She reached for the switch, but he took her arm and pulled her close to him, his lips seeking hers.

"No, we don't need the light." Dinner was left for later as he swept her into his muscled arms and carried her up the stairs.

Chapter Twenty-Five

Nick rose before daybreak to go to the bathroom. He passed Casey's room, sneering at the loud snoring. In the moonlight that flooded the room through open curtains, he could see Casey. He had one arm hanging across his chest while the other lay across his forehead. He paused watching Casey's chest rise with each breath he took. As if he knew he was being watched, he flipped over, his back to the door.

Nick returned to his room and collected his gun and hunting knife from his bag. Sleep had evaded him for most of the night as his mind churned with the task that lay before him. His thoughts had also been on Rebecca. By now, there would no doubt be questions about her not showing up for work. He would have to move quickly, before Danes tied her disappearance to him and moved Sophia again.

He checked the pistol, making sure each chamber had a bullet, but he hoped not to have to use the gun. His weapon of choice was his knife with the serrated edge. Pulling the knife from its brown leather sheath, he traced the blade across the palm of his hand. A thin line of blood appeared across his hand. With a malicious grin, he placed the knife back in its sheath.

Nick carried the weapons into the living room and laid them on the table. He fixed himself a cup of coffee.

Casey snorted and flopped over in the bed, facing the door now. Nick shook his head. Casey was letting his impatience make him careless.

What if Sophia had been looking out a window and seen him as he rode toward the lake? She could have easily caught sight of his face and recognized him. All he was supposed to do was snoop around and leave while staying within the shadows of the trees as much as possible. And he was drinking more, too. Alcohol made Casey crazy and loosened his tongue. Nick believed Casey might just be a liability to him now.

He threw a couple logs on the fire and breathed in the hickory smoke that filled the chimney. He pulled one of the wooden ladderback chairs near the hearth to finish his coffee. He watched the red embers glow and then fade away to ash, much as Sophia's love for him had.

Sophia. A beautiful woman, with her auburn hair and green eyes, yet he never fell in love with her as she did him. She had only been a challenge to him. Someone to conquer after she spurned his request for her address and phone number. His friends told him how lucky he was to have Sophia, but he disagreed. She was the lucky one.

He did marry her, and he had to admit he did like being with her—until she talked about having a baby. What did he need with a baby? Someone to take Sophia's mind off him? He had let her know that there would be no baby, and he had let her know in a way she wouldn't forget. She didn't speak of it again.

Then that night…

He had come home earlier than usual. Sophia wanted to talk to him, but he hadn't wanted to talk. He went to the garage. She followed him to the garage, something she never did, asking him to just talk to her for a few minutes.

He had disregarded her and her whining until she tripped on a tool chest. She caught herself from falling, but in doing so, she grabbed a small yellow tote that sat on his work bench and spilt the contents across the floor. He had exploded and grabbed her, slapping her hard across the face, and then his hands had slipped to her neck. With her fingers hooked on his, she gasped and begged him to stop, a look of pure fear on her face. She just wanted to…what? When he let go, he shoved her out of the garage before she could see that the tote had fake IDs and old license plates stored inside.

The next evening, she was gone. He didn't really care until he found his duffle bag with the key hidden in it was gone, too. Thunderous anger shook his entire body. He regretted not choking the life out of her when he had her in his grasp the night before.

Sighing, Nick finished his coffee and went back to bed. Casey had now flipped onto his stomach. *Sleep on, Casey.* Everything was ready. His plans were laid.

Chapter Twenty-Six

Feeling hot, Sophia flipped the cover off and opened her eyes. It was early morning, not dawn yet. She slid her legs over the side of the bed, feeling the familiar sickness rise in her throat, but now her head throbbed. She tiptoed to the bathroom and faced the toilet bowl, sick once more.

In the mirror, she was ashen with dark circles under her eyes. She splashed water on her face and reached for the door, but another wave hit her like a bomb. This wasn't just morning sickness. She was sick. Please don't let me have the flu, she prayed.

"Roman," Sophia whispered when she returned to the bed. She gently shook his shoulder. With a grunt, he opened his eyes.

"Sophia, what's wrong?" he mumbled groggily, sitting up in the bed.

"I don't know. I'm still throwing up, but now I've got a nasty headache. I'm going to get something to drink. Do we have any medicine?"

"I'll check." Roman grabbed his robe and followed her down the stairs. "Go and lie down on the couch, and I'll get whatever you need." Thankful for his help, she lay down. She could hear him rattling around in the kitchen. He came back with a glass of Sprite, but as soon as the liquid hit her stomach, she ran for the bathroom.

When she came out, Roman watched her cross the room, his eyebrows drawn together.

"We don't have any medicine, but I'm really worried about you. As soon as it's daylight, I'm going to the reservation to get you some help. Jon's mother is a shaman. She'll know what to do. I'll let Helen and Otis know, too."

Relieved, she lay back on the throw pillow and closed her eyes, flitting in and out of chaotic dreams. She was holding her mom's hands and dancing around the living room on the old blue and white flowered rug. Next, she was in the car with her dad as he tried to teach her to drive. Then she was with Nick as he proposed, the Nick she had fallen in love with, but who had quickly turned into the Nick that left cuts and bruises. Suddenly, she jerked awake and sat up with a scream.

"I'm here," Roman said softly from his perch beside her on the floor. "You've had a bad dream."

"Yeah, I did," she agreed, thankful it was only a dream. "What time is it?" She saw daylight through the windows.

"It's almost ten."

"I've slept for a long time."

"If you think you'll be okay, I'm going to run out to the reservation to get Jon and Maggie."

"I'll be fine. The headache and nausea has eased off." Roman got to his feet and reached around to the coffee table and picked up the pistol. After snapping the safety off, he laid it on her lap.

"You know what to do if you need to use this. I'll be back as soon as I can."

Sophia watched as he donned his coat and gloves. He locked the door, but she set the gun aside and padded to the door to set the latch. She lay back down, pondering on everything that Roman had told her last night. At last, she dozed off.

Chapter Twenty-Seven

It was full daylight when Nick woke up. He jumped from the bed and dressed. He hadn't meant to fall asleep. Looking at his watch, he swore silently. 9:00 a.m. He grabbed his boots and went into the kitchen. Casey was sitting at the table, drinking coffee and rubbing his eyes.

"Been up long?" Nick asked, sitting across from him and leaning over to put his boots on.

"Not too long." Casey yawned.

"Any more coffee?"

"Help yourself."

Nick poured a cup of coffee and sat back down, sipping the strong brew. Casey stared at his cup, spinning his spoon on the table.

"What's on your mind?" Nick asked, rubbing his forehead. The scraping of the spoon was wearing on his already hyped-up nerves.

"I was just wondering when we're going to make our move. Quite frankly, I'm ready to get the hell out of Dodge."

"Today," Nick answered, his face getting red. But Casey didn't seem to notice.

"Good. I've waited long enough to get what's due me when we get the key." Casey pushed back from the table and disappeared into his room. When he returned, he had his pistol and a cloth in his hand. Sitting back down at the table, he wiped the gun down. When he had it spit shined, he took several bullets from his shirt pocket and loaded the chambers.

"I don't know about that."

"What's to know?" Casey's voice was cold. "We get the key and then head out to collect what's ours."

"We may have to wait till things cool off, or at best make sure we aren't being followed. We sure don't need to get caught with the goods."

"No damn way!" Casey shouted and began to pace around the room, waving his arms. "We need to strike while the iron is hot. When we get the key, we hightail it out of here and go straight to Georgia. We've waited, or at least I've waited, far too long. It's always *wait* with you. Wait until you say it's time. We waited for you to get information from that girl and look how long that took, and we still ended up having to break in and then kill her."

"Yeah, I had to move slowly. You knew the risk I was taking. And there seems to always be people with Sophia. You've seen that," Nick shouted back, rising to his feet and kicking the wooden chair into the fridge. "It has to be timed right."

"Bull. Just go to the cabin and kill everyone there. Then we get out of town, you give me what's due me, and I'll hop on down to Mexico!" Casey stuck his gun in his waistband. "And, by the way, I want a bigger share."

"We have an agreement," Nick replied curtly, trying to rein in his anger and glaring at Casey with smoldering eyes.

"We *had* an agreement. You forget that I know everything. And I do all the dirty work. I want a fifty-fifty share. Remember, if I go to the police, your life is over. I know I'd spend time, but not as long as you if I get a plea deal."

Nick caught the implication. He turned his back to Casey and strode into the bathroom. What had gotten into Casey? Fear? Greed? He wondered if Casey might try to kill him and take the key. Yeah, he was sure he would try to kill him.

Looking at his face in the mirror, Nick made an uneasy decision. He couldn't risk Casey leading the police to him. He had always been erratic and a lone wolf, but he had been able to control him—until now. He had just become a liability.

Casey was standing in front of the large window by the front door, his hands shoved into his pockets, when Nick emerged from the bathroom. He ducked into his room and, in seconds, returned to the living room with his hunting knife in hand. He slipped up behind Casey. He turned his head slightly, but before he could react, Nick grabbed a handful of hair and jerked his head back. He pulled the knife across Casey's throat. Blood squirted and immediately flowed down his chest.

As Casey grabbed at his throat, he stared at Nick in wide-eyed surprise. Nick dragged him out of the door and onto the frozen ground and then knelt beside him, as Casey struggled against death.

"Well, I thought it over, and you're right. You do know everything. Too much, in fact. So, I gave you what you had coming to you. How dare you blackmail me?" But Nick was now talking to a dead man. Casey's eyes rolled back in his head, and his bloody hands fell limply to his side.

Nick found a tarp in the small garage and rolled Casey's bloody body in it and strapped it to the ATV. He cleaned the cabin and then, after cleaning his knife, he slid it into the sheath and shoved his pistol in his coat pocket. He would dump Casey's body in the lake and then go to the cabin where Sophia was. He would kill her, get the key, come back here to gather his things, and then take off for the airport.

Driving the ATV through the woods, he circled around to the lake. Fortunately, he saw no one else. He dragged Casey's body to the water and flipped it into the frigid water and watched as the water rippled and bubbled until the body disappeared into the depths.

Back on the ATV, Nick drove back through the woods toward Danes' cabin, stopping behind a dense area of brush near the shed, and hid the ATV. Silently, he slipped inside the shed, his knife in hand, to look around. He was relieved to see the snowmobile gone. After checking out the shed and heading back to the door, he heard shuffling and looked up to see that a man had crept up behind him wearing a heavy jacket and a ski mask. Without hesitating, Nick plunged the knife into the man's exposed throat and jerked it out with one smooth move. The man grabbed for the slit in his throat but fell to the floor with a thump.

With the point of the knife, he pulled back the mask and grunted. Bending over, he wiped the bloody knife on the dead man's jacket.

Nick snaked his way from the shed to the cabin and hurried around to the side where the kitchen door was. A couple of the panes were broken. Pieces of wood covered the holes, but looking through one of the small windowpanes, he could just see the top of Sophia's head lying on a pillow against the couch arm. The fire was dying down, so he thought she was probably sleeping, but he wanted to get a better look. He slipped around the cabin and stood with his back to the chimney, leaning toward the window to peer in.

Sophia was lying on her side asleep. Her right arm was curled under the pillow while her left hand was snuggled against her breast. He saw no one else in the room. He smiled wickedly. Almost there, he thought. Then he glanced at the front door. Wooden with a lock and a latch. The kitchen door had two locks: a key lock and a chain lock. He considered his options.

Silently, he stepped up onto the porch and pulled out a small red case with the initial C on the back printed in black marker. Casey had taught Nick how to pick locks with these very tools. Quickly he found the tool he needed and inserted it into the keyhole. It only took a moment before the tumbler turned.

Chapter Twenty-Eight

Sophia, only half asleep, heard the key in the lock. Roman's back, she thought and groggily lifted the latch and turned the doorknob to let him in. But when the door swung open, she shuddered and screamed loudly, throwing her body against the door, trying to close it. With a cruel grin on his face, Nick shoved his foot in the gap between the door and the frame.

"Get out, get out!" Sophia screamed. Fully awake now, and her heart racing, she gasped for breath.

Sophia was no match for Nick, who easily shoved the door open and thrust her backward. Whirling around, Sophia rushed toward the stairs, terrified. As her foot touched the first step, Nick grabbed her hair and jerked her back to him, spinning her around to face him. He grabbed her arms and squeezed.

"Found you at last." He snarled, lowering his face to hers. She tried to pull away but he held her close. "I want my key!" he screamed in her face, shaking her.

"I don't know what you're talking about!" Defiantly she tried to free her arms and fight back. He pressed her arms behind her back and forced her down on the floor, sitting astride her chest.

"Where's my duffle bag?"

"Get off me!" She writhed under him, trying to free herself. His weight was making it difficult for her to breathe.

"Give me my key, or I'll kill you," he hissed in her ear.

"I don't know—"

Suddenly, the weight was lifted as she heard Roman's voice bellow out, "Get off her!" Roman grabbed him by his coat and flung him across the room.

Gasping for air, she pulled herself up as Nick stumbled backward across the room, slamming into the wall. Pushing off the wall, Nick jerked his knife from the sheath and lunged at Roman. Roman searched frantically for a weapon but had no time to grab anything. With the force of Nick's attack, both men stumbled backward, crashing into the kitchen wall and then rolling on the floor until Nick got an opportunity to plunge the knife into Roman's shoulder.

Screaming out Roman's name, Sophia ran to the couch and grabbed the pistol, aiming it at Nick who was about to stab Roman again.

"Nick!" she shrieked. "Leave him alone."

Nick slowly turned to face her, the bloody knife in his hand and a smirk on his face. "Put the gun down, Sophia."

"I'll kill you!" she shouted, tears running down her cheeks. "I swear I will."

"No, you won't. Look at you shake." He walked toward her, brandishing the knife. "You don't have the backbone," he said, continuing to close in on her. Suddenly he stopped and raised an eyebrow.

"What? You're pregnant. You didn't tell me I was going to be a dad," he said sarcastically.

Sophia silently stared at Nick, keeping the gun aimed at him.

"It is mine, right?" Sophia remained silent, her finger on the trigger. "Or maybe not. It doesn't matter. All I want is the key."

Sophia slowly retreated until her back was against the bookshelf. She had no idea what key he was talking about. But was he right? Could she kill him? She was shaking badly, but for her child and Roman, she would die trying. Keeping her eye on Nick, she watched him step closer.

"I will shoot you," she said, steadying her hand. Behind Nick, she saw Roman move. He was alive, and that gave her strength. Then she grimaced when she heard Roman moan. Nick turned around in time to see Roman shift his body around.

"I'm gonna kill you and then him. He can watch you die," he hissed and lunged at her. An explosion shattered in the air, and Nick stopped moving. His eyes looked at her in disbelief as a red stain spread across his coat. Blood gurgled from his mouth and down his chin as he dropped to his knees. The knife clanged to the floor. Sophia rushed to the knife and kicked it across the room. Then he fell forward, his head smacking the floor, and lay still.

Sophia ran to Roman, screaming out his name. He was lying motionless now, blood everywhere. Dropping the gun, she ran for towels, wondering how she would get him help. Then she remembered the ATV. Packing the towels on the gaping wound, she would ride to…where? She wasn't sure where Helen and Otis lived, or anyone else for that matter, but she had to get help. Packing more towels on the wound, she felt his phone in his shirt pocket.

"Please work," she prayed as she tried the phone, but

still no service. In angry desperation, she threw the phone and sobbed. But she was determined to save him. She reached under him to move him to the couch, praying for strength.

"Sophia, wait." Jon Light Heels ran into the room, an elderly woman behind him. After a hurried look around the room, he rushed to her.

"Oh, Jon, thank God you're here. Please help him." She wept uncontrollably. "How did you know?"

"Roman came to us and said you were sick. Mom came to check on you." He nodded at the elderly woman. Sophia had momentarily forgotten that Roman had left to get help for her. "How bad is it?"

"Pretty bad. He's lost a lot of blood. Please help him," Sophia pleaded again. Kneeling beside him, she touched his cheek.

The elderly lady stepped up. "Jon, put him in bed," she ordered.

In one swift motion, Jon picked Roman up and carried him upstairs to his room. The woman followed with Sophia on her heels. She paused and turned to Sophia.

"Come closer, child," she said in a smooth tone, motioning for Sophia with a wrinkled hand. Sophia moved closer. The woman laid her hands on each side of Sophia's stomach and closed her eyes. "The child is well, but you must stay down here. You are in shock, and I need to tend to Roman's wound without interruption."

"No, please," she begged, wringing her hands and shaking her head hysterically. "I promise I won't be in the way."

The woman nodded, relenting, and hurried up the steps. "My name is Maggie."

165

Sophia followed her into the room. "You sit there and don't move unless I tell you to." Maggie pointed a crooked finger at the chair next to the window. "Jon will get the things I need."

Sitting, Sophia nervously twisted her hands together and silently prayed as she stared at Roman's ashen face. Maggie worked feverishly, spitting out orders to Jon. After two pots of hot water, bandages, and gauze were obtained, Maggie gave Jon an order in their native language and continued to work. Jon nodded and disappeared, returning about thirty minutes later. When he reappeared, he spoke to Maggie again in their native language. Maggie motioned for Sophia.

"I have done all I can for him, but he needs to rest. Let's go downstairs and take care of you."

"But I really want to stay with him," She pleaded with Maggie.

"I know you do, but I really need to check you out, too. Jon will stay with Roman, and then you can be with him later."

Reluctantly, Sophia nodded, and with a last glance at Roman, who was lying very still and pale on the checkered quilt, she followed Maggie downstairs and sat down beside her on the couch. Nick's body was gone. That must have been what they were talking about in their language. Suddenly, feeling weak and nauseated, she dropped her head in her hands. She shivered.

"Please lie down," Maggie coaxed when Sophia resisted. She gave in and Maggie covered her with a throw, but she instantly shot up when the door was thrown open again. Relieved to see Helen and Otis were standing there, she rushed to Helen and threw her arms around her, and in a rush of words and pointing up to the bedroom, she tried to tell Helen everything at once.

Helen guided her back to the couch with soothing words and caressing her hair, telling her that everything would be all right. "Sit back and I will take care of you."

"But what if Roman dies? He's hurt so bad," Sophia cried out. Otis was at the wood box, looking out the window. Sophia could see his broad shoulders shaking as Maggie disappeared into the kitchen.

"Now you listen to me. We won't think that way. Maggie knows what she is doing and is a very good medicine woman. Roman will get through this, and so will you." Helen pulled Sophia close and rocked her.

"Sophia, drink this," Maggie ordered, returning from the kitchen. Sophia pressed her lips together in a thin line, refusing.

Helen gently urged her to drink. "Honey, drink this," taking the glass from Maggie. "It will only relax you." Sophia took the glass and drank down the cool but bitter liquid. The last thing Sophia remembered was Helen's comforting smile and a cool rag on her forehead.

Chapter Twenty-Nine

Sophia opened her eyes and sat up. Remembering the previous events, she was determined to see Roman. Running her fingers through her hair, she prepared to rise, but then she saw him sitting in the rocking chair next to the fireplace, his chin resting on his bare chest, breathing softly. Gauze and bandages were wrapped thickly around his shoulder. Near his feet, Maggie was sleeping on a quilt next to the hearth. Sophia flinched at the unexpected touch on her shoulder.

"Sophia, are you okay?" Helen whispered.

"Yeah, I am, but what's all of this?" Sophia waved her hand around the room. "Shouldn't Roman be in bed resting?"

"Can you stand up and walk to the kitchen?" Helen asked, still whispering.

"Yeah. I feel a little shaky, but I can." Slowly, Sophia followed Helen into the kitchen. "What's going on? How long have I been sleeping?"

"You've been asleep about thirteen hours."

"No way."

"Yes, dear. Maggie gave you an herb to make you relax and sleep. You were in shock last night, and we didn't want you to lose the baby from the stress. As soon as Roman woke up, which was only a couple of hours ago, he insisted on coming down here to be by your side."

"What about Otis and Jon?" Sophia asked.

"They left a while ago with Sheriff Raines. They've been in touch with Mr. Danes, and they are checking out the Kellers' cabin."

Sophia sat down, not knowing what to say. Her heart swelled with love for Roman and the idea that he wanted to stay down here with her, but she felt he would heal faster if he were in bed. She said as much to Helen. Helen set a cup of coffee in front of her. Sophia reached for the cup, but a dark shadow crossed her face.

"What about Nick's body? I know Jon took it out last night."

Inhaling deeply, Helen walked over to Sophia and put her hand on her shoulder and kissed the top of Sophia's messy hair. "Jon wrapped the body in a tarp and put it in the shed. I'm so sorry all this has happened to you."

"Oh, Helen, I'm the one that's caused trouble for all of you, and for Roman."

"Nonsense. Now go and shower while I fix breakfast."

Sophia took a few steps, then paused and looked back. "How did you guys know to come out here?"

"Roman stopped by to give us an update on the break-in at Mr. Danes' office. We decided to finish what we were doing and pack some things to stay with you for a few days to help keep you safe and secure, but unfortunately, we came too late."

"No, you didn't." Sophia shook her head. "You might have been hurt too."

"Now scoot along," Helen ordered with moist eyes.

****

Sophia emerged a short time later. She paused on the landing when she heard an unfamiliar voice downstairs. Looking over the railing, she saw the sheriff leaning against the wall next to the wood box and talking to Roman, a cup of coffee in his hand. Jon and Otis were beside Roman on the couch. Hill had arrived and was hunkered down in front of the fire, poking a stick in the grate. A deputy was standing guard in front of the door, his feet apart with his thumbs hooked over his utility belt. Hill suddenly looked up and glared at her, his face tight and red. She felt a chill as their eyes locked.

Roman looked up also. He motioned for her to come down. At the bottom of the stairs, he met her. Otis took a seat in the rocking chair, and Jon went to stand next to the sheriff to make room for her on the couch. Helen and Maggie joined them. Hill spun around but remained crouched, his cold eyes making her uneasy.

"Roman?"

"Sophia, this is Sheriff Raines and his deputy, Tony Williams."

"Yes, Helen told me you were coming out. I'll help in any way I can." Sophia shook the sheriff's hand, and she felt Helen pat her back when she sat down between her and Roman.

"I've told him all I know, but he has questions for you." Roman took her hand and squeezed it.

Sophia listened intently to his questions, answering them as best she could, walking him through what had happened.

"Well, I'm convinced that what happened was self-defense on your part. That's what will be in my report, so no charges will be forthcoming."

"Thank you, Sheriff, but what about Nick's cousin

Casey? Has he been arrested?" She caught the quick glance between Roman and the sheriff.

"Unfortunately, no. We believe Nick killed him. We know they were staying at the Kellers' together, but no sign could be found of Casey. A small amount of blood was found in the cabin and next to the porch. We've sent blood samples to the lab, but it'll be a couple days before the tests are back. And we are getting a team to drag the lake, but that's all I can tell you."

"Thank you. I hope I've been of some help." She started to get up, but Roman took her hand.

"Sophia, there's one more thing you need to know." Roman sighed, glancing swiftly at Hill. From the pained look on his face, Sophia knew more bad news was coming her way. She steeled herself, but she wondered just how much more bad news she could take. "Nick killed Jasper. Jon found his body in the shed when he took Nick's out there. We think Jasper surprised him and Nick killed him. Jasper had no defensive wounds, so Nick attacked without warning."

Sophia gasped out loud. The world was spinning out of control. She felt Roman's arm on her shoulders. She certainly hadn't liked Jasper, but...

"Hill, I'm so sorry. I don't even know what to say. I've caused so much pain," she said, feeling everyone's eyes on her. She briefly wondered if her life would be without pain again.

"Don't say anything. I don't want to hear it. I'm only up here to get his body," he said gruffly and spit into the fireplace. The hot log sizzled as Hill strode out the door and disappeared.

Sophia, not knowing what else to say, slipped her hands from Roman's, but he reached out to her close to him. She had cost people their lives and ruined many more by consenting to come up here. She could no longer remain here in the place where she had caused so much suffering. Now that Nick was dead, she could leave and let people heal.

"Roman, we're leaving now. Don't hesitate to get us if you need us." Sheriff Raines nodded at his deputy, and they left quickly. In a moment's time, Sophia heard the sheriff's truck start up, and the pair drove away.

Jon followed the two men outside, and Otis and Maggie followed Helen into the kitchen. Sophia pulled away from Roman and headed toward the stairs.

"Where are you going?" Roman called after her and hurried to catch her. Her hand was on the banister when he gently grasped her arm. "This Nick thing is over now. You can relax. Everything will be okay."

"How can you even look at me after all the lives I've ruined? Rebecca and Jasper were killed because of me, and you were almost killed and Hill hates me and will eventually hate you. It's all my fault!" she cried out, her voice shrill. Before he could answer, she fled up the stairs. In her room, she stood in front of the window staring at the mountains. She had no more tears to cry, yet her heart was broken. She continued to stare out the window as the door gently opened and closed. "Roman, I love you, but I have to go away. Please understand. I don't want to hurt anyone else. I need to go where no one knows me and start over." She twisted her shirt between her fingers.

"Roman loves you, too. You shouldn't run from him." Maggie's soft voice filled the room. Startled, Sophia wheeled around. "It's not your fault. Nick didn't have to do what he did. I understand how you feel about

172

Rebecca and Jasper, but again, that was out of your control. You know that Jasper saved Roman's hide from me when Raven died, but Jasper slinked around in places he shouldn't. I believe, as does Jon, he was snooping around when he ran into Nick."

Sophia felt some of the guilt and grief lift off her. "But I don't want to come between Roman and Hill. They're great friends, and Hill will always resent me."

Maggie chuckled. "Many women have come between good friends, but you won't. In time, Hill will come around and see that you're not to blame. I know Hill pretty well, and I promise it won't take him long. And please believe me when I say that I can see the love Roman has for you."

"Thank you."

"Welcome. Now, I can hear your stomach growling. Your child is hungry, and so am I." When Maggie opened the door, Roman was standing there, pale, his face twisted with worry. Without saying a word, Sophia moved into his embrace. He took her chin and tilted her head back. Sophia felt Maggie sweep past her while Roman passionately kissed her willing lips.

Chapter Thirty

Silence. Everyone was gone. Sophia smiled up at Roman when he sat beside her on the couch and put his good arm around her. She laid her head against his shoulder. Against the darkening night, the fire burned brightly and cheerfully. She wanted to ask when they would be leaving for Tennessee, but the tranquility and quiet of the last several hours was too good to mess up with talking.

Peace. Nick was dead. No longer would she have to peer over her shoulder wondering if or when he would be there. Maybe she should feel some loss for her baby's sake, but she didn't. There were a few good memories, but mostly there were bad ones. Both the good and bad memories would be buried, never to be resurrected again. He had hunted her down, even changing his appearance, but she knew…

"Roman." She rose from her comfortable place. A thought, a memory, had surfaced.

With a new look of concern, he asked, "What's wrong?"

"Nothing's wrong. It's just that Nick said something to me, and I've just remembered it."

"Sophia, let it go."

"No. I really think it's important." Sweeping her hair back from her face, she looked at him, perplexed.

"What is it?"

"Remember you said I might know something that I didn't think was important? I don't think Nick was after me, per se. But he said there was something I had that he wanted back."

Roman's eyes narrowed, and she could see that his investigator interest was piqued. "Go on," he urged her.

"Before you came rushing in, he was yelling something about a key and how I took his duffle bag and he wanted it back."

"Do you have the duffle bag? I didn't pay a lot of attention to your luggage when we arrived here."

"Yeah. I needed it to throw clothes in when I left Georgia, and then I used it for the trip here."

"Nick didn't come here because you took his duffle bag, but it makes sense if something is in it. Did you say he was yelling about a key?"

"Yeah." She nodded her head.

"We need to look the bag over. Will you get it?"

"Be right back." Sophia was about to ascend the stairs when she heard a loud rap on the door. She returned to stand by Roman when he got up to answer it. Nervously, she held her breath, not wanting their peaceful night shattered by more bad news. The door swung open, and Hill stood on the threshold.

"Hill, come in." Roman held the door as the tall man stepped inside and removed his furry aviator's hat.

"Thanks."

"What's up?" Roman asked, waving his hand toward a chair.

"Well, I, uh, wanted to apologize to Sophia for what I said earlier." Sophia watched him twist his hat in his hands. She realized that apologies were hard for him, but he was trying. "Jasper was my only brother, but he was always snooping around where he didn't belong, and that's probably what got him killed. It doesn't lessen the hurt, but it's not your fault by any means. I'm sorry."

"No apologies needed." She went over to him and, standing on her tiptoes, gave him a hug. "Can I get you some coffee? I have some made."

"No, I'm good, thank you." He held up his hand and sat down in the rocking chair. "By the way, Roman, I called Rosemary and told her about Jasper."

"How'd she take it?"

"Pretty good, although she won't be coming out for the service. But you remember when Jasper accused her of taking…" He paused, his voice tight, and his eyes glancing over at Sophia.

"Sophia knows about Jasper and Rosemary," Roman interjected. Nodding, Hill continued.

"I went to the garage after I left here, just to think, and I was moving things around and pulling out drawers, you know, just making busy work and thinking about Jasper."

"Yeah." Roman nodded.

"Well, I found these tucked away in his desk drawer." He reached into his pocket and pulled out five coins and handed them to Roman.

"Coins from your parents' collection?" Roman whistled, turning them over in his hand.

"Yeah. Jasper took those coins and blamed Rosemary. He's probably been systematically selling them off."

"Oh, Hill, I'm so sorry," Sophia exclaimed, seeing the pain in his eyes.

"You're going to tell Rosemary, aren't you?"

Roman handed the coins back to Hill.

"Yeah, but I'm going to take some time and go see her. Tell her in person." He licked his lips. "And, Sophia, a cup of coffee would be good now."

"I'll be back in a minute." Sophia hurried to the kitchen, with Roman behind her.

"I was thinking that maybe we could get Hill to help with the duffle bag mystery. Take his mind off things for the night. What do you think?"

"Okay with me, but I don't think it'll amount to much."

"If you'll go get the bag, I'll take this to Hill and bring him up to speed."

Upstairs, she pulled the black bag from the closet and opened it. A T-shirt and a pair of socks were still in it. She threw the clothes on the bed and took the empty bag down, handing it to Roman.

"I explained everything to Hill, and he thinks it's interesting too," Roman said, picking up the bag and turning it inside out. Sophia leaned toward Roman, watching anxiously, as did Hill. he checked the bag thoroughly, even the zippered pouches. Nothing. Turning it upside down, he shook it vigorously, but nothing fell out except a piece of lint.

"Well," Roman muttered and returned the bag to its original state, letting it drop to the floor at his feet.

"Sophia, do you think that in your state of panic you misunderstood Nick?" Hill asked, staring at the bag.

"No. I remember thinking, why would he follow me all the way here for his duffle bag? And then he was shouting about a key."

"Do you remember throwing anything away from it? Anything that might have had a key in it?" Roman asked, chewing his lip.

"No, but the whole thing is weird," Sophia mused. She bent over to pick up the bag and take it back upstairs when Roman reached for it.

"Wait. Hill, can I have your knife?"

"Sure." He handed Roman a large hunting knife from a sheath that was hanging on his belt. While Hill held the bag, Roman cut along the bottom of the bag until he had cut the entire length.

"The leather's been cut and glued around the edge so well that it was hardly noticeable," Roman explained as he peeled back the leather, revealing a concealed cavity. Sophia inhaled sharply when a small yellow envelope fell out. As he opened the envelope, a gold key fell out into his hand. He held it up for them to see.

"Oh, my gosh! There is a key," Sophia yelped, moving closer to look at it.

"Do you recognize it?" Roman asked, turning it around.

"No."

"Are you sure?"

"On that I am. I…" Sophia hesitated, struggling to continue. "I would search through his truck, dresser drawers, and once even his wallet when I had the chance. I had gotten where I didn't trust him, so I wanted to see what he was up to, but I never saw that key," she explained, feeling her cheeks burn at her admission.

"Maybe a bank box?" Roman asked. Sophia shook her head and shrugged her shoulders.

"Is there anything else inside the envelope?" Hill asked. Roman stuck his finger in the envelope and pulled out a small, folded slip of paper. After reading what was on the paper, Roman turned to Sophia.

"There's an address on it with a number. 105. Maybe for a bank in Atlanta."

"If Nick had a bank account or safe deposit box, I never knew about it," Sophia said. "Jeez, he wouldn't even talk about us having a checking account or a credit card."

"But, if it's a key to a safe deposit box, why go through all this trouble? Why not have the bank issue a new one?" Hill asked, rubbing his chin. "I've never had one, so I'm not sure how that would work."

"You have a point. Yeah, he could have had the bank issue a new key." Roman frowned. "And if there were a bank box, Sophia, you would certainly have seen something about it. There are fees, which mean paper trails, not to mention Uncle Ralph would certainly have uncovered something during the divorce, unless of course, he's using someone else's."

"But then again, just have the bank make a new one," Sophia said. She was beginning to see just how deceiving Nick truly had been. She hadn't known him at all and wondered what they would discover when they finally did figure out the mystery of the key. Did she really want to know?

"Hill, how soon can you get us to the airport?"

"As soon as you need me to."

"Okay. Pick us up about six. We'll go into town, and I'll call and get us a flight."

"I'll be here."

"We'll be ready." Roman shook his friend's hand as he started to leave. "Hill, wait. Why don't you fly down with us and stay a few days? You can help us and then go on to visit Rosemary."

Grinning, Hill slipped his hat back on and replied,

"Just might do that, buddy." The door swung open, and Hill was gone.

"Ready to go home?" Roman wrapped her in his arms, his lips softly kissing her neck.

"Yeah," she whispered, holding him tightly, feeling happy. A part of her wanted to scream no, that she wanted to stay here forever, but she knew that wasn't possible.

Chapter Thirty-One

Sophia, Roman, and Hill disembarked from the airplane at the Nashville Airport. Sophia, taking in the Music City's advertisements, followed the two men across the concourse and down the escalator to the baggage carousels. Extracting their bags from the belt, Roman led the way to the exit, where a rental was waiting for them. Sophia was impressed by the black BMW he had rented.

"Hey, I'm hungry. What about you two?" Roman asked after maneuvering through the heavy Nashville traffic, heading east toward Spring City.

"Yeah. Those plane peanuts didn't last," Hill joked.

"I am, too. There are several restaurants at Pleasant Pointe Mall. That's just a few miles ahead," Sophia offered.

Roman darted off the interstate and onto the off ramp. After circling the mall and barely avoiding a fender bender at a stop sign, he parked in front of a steak house. An hour and a half later, they were on the road again. Sophia closed her eyes until they arrived back in Spring City, where Roman drove directly to the law office.

"Hey, Nicole," Roman called out to the beautiful blonde-haired woman sitting at the seat that Rebecca had previously occupied as the trio passed through the lobby.

Sophia felt a spike of guilt remembering the redhead who had sat there. She and Hill followed Roman through the lobby and into the inner office, pausing at Nicole's desk. She stood up, taking off her headset.

"Nicole, you remember Sophia, and this is my good friend, Hill Masters. Hill, this is Nicole."

"Nice to meet you, Hill," Nicole said, offering her hand. Then she turned toward Sophia.

Was it her imagination, or did Nicole eye her suspiciously? Did she blame Sophia for Rebecca's death? Sophia tensed when Nicole came out from behind the desk but relaxed when she took her hands into her well-manicured ones, asking if she was okay. Sophia tilted her head slightly back, deeply inhaling Nicole's perfume.

"I'm well, thank you."

"Mr. Danes is on his way in. You can wait in his office." Roman thanked her and headed down the hallway with Sophia in tow.

"You coming, Hill?" Roman looked back.

"I think I'll watch Nicole type, if it's all right with her?" Hill smiled at the receptionist. Nicole nodded, pulling up a chair. Roman chuckled, leaving his friend alone with her.

"Hey, why were you sniffing the air?"

"Calvin Klein perfume. I love it." Sophia laughed softly.

Caressing her cheek, Roman kissed her lightly but quickly pulled back when Mr. Danes walked in.

"Uncle Ralph," Roman exclaimed, intending to hug the large man. Mr. Danes pushed Roman aside and stepped toward Sophia, taking her hand, leaving Roman with a perplexed look.

"Sophia, I'm so relieved that you are okay. How do you feel?"

"I'm good."

"And Roman, your friend is out there flirting with my secretary." Danes raised his eyebrows at his nephew.

"I know, but what can I say?" Roman raised his hands, palms up. Sophia caught Mr. Danes rolling his eyes at Roman.

"Anyway, we need to discuss a few things, and then I think you guys have some sleuthing to do." Sophia glanced at Roman, who was grinning widely at her.

"Yes, sir," she responded, sitting in the familiar chair he offered her.

For the next thirty minutes, she and Roman brought him up to date on all that had happened, filling in the gaps he didn't know about. Mr. Danes didn't interrupt but occasionally nodded his head, wrote on the legal pad, or uttered a soft uh-huh. Once in a while, he glanced up at Sophia.

Sophia kept up with the conversation for a while but was soon lost in her own thoughts as Roman took over. Unconsciously, she placed her hand lovingly over her stomach. She thought of Helen and the baby blanket she had given her. Roman had told Hill to drive by their farm so she could say goodbye. Both women had cried and hugged, but Roman had promised enthusiastically that they would return after the baby was old enough to travel. Otis had given Roman a stern order to watch over Sophia, and then he hugged her with misty eyes.

Her thoughts were interrupted when she heard the name Casey. Roman asked if she wanted to hear all that was coming. She nodded. Mr. Danes continued.

"I received a call this morning from Sheriff Raines.

183

Crescent Lake was dragged, and a body wrapped in a tarp was found. It was Casey's. His throat had been slit." Danes paused, drawing a breath. Looking away, Sophia felt her stomach tighten.

"Sophia, are you okay?" Roman leaned toward her, taking her arm. "You're white as a sheet."

"I'm okay," she replied, pushing down the urge to throw up. "Casey probably double-crossed Nick." There was another one to add to his list of victims. She wondered how she could have married such an evil man.

"Anyway, Sophia, the police did find your apartment trashed. It's been cleaned and repaired, but I thought that you might want another apartment, so Nicole found one on Lennox Avenue beside—"

"She's going to stay at my apartment for a while." Seeing that Roman's mind was already made up on that point, Mr. Danes continued.

"That's all I have, except for the baby. I had already gotten ready for proceedings, but since Nick is dead, nothing else needs to be done. Is there anything else I can help you with, or do you need anything?"

"Thank you, but I'll be fine. All I need is a job and a car."

"Don't worry, Sophia, I know good things will come your way." He patted her on the back as she and Roman left his office.

"Come on, Casanova, we've got to travel," Roman said, pulling Hill away from Nicole and out the door. Sophia saw Nicole slip Hill a folded piece of paper, which he promptly stuck in his pocket.

"What's on the agenda now?" Hill asked, sliding his long torso into the back seat of the BMW, letting Sophia have the front.

"Get my car from the apartment and take this car back to the rental place. They have a shop in town."

Roman headed north out of town and to the Deerwood Apartments. When they got there, Hill jumped out of the BMW after Roman tossed him the keys to his Dodge Charger. "You drive my car and follow me to the rental agency." Again, they headed back to town and down Jefferson Avenue.

"What about my car?" Sophia asked, watching the familiar scenery pass.

"Uncle Ralph had it put in storage. What kind of car do you have?"

"A Camaro. Candy apple red. It's an older car, but I've had it forever and it ran well, that is until…"

"It's okay, Sophia. You can talk about it if you want to."

"Nick nearly ran it into the ground. He had a truck, but he liked keeping mine on the road, taking long drives to put more useless miles on it, revving the motor until I thought it would blow up, racing it and laughing at me when I pleaded with him to stop." Her voice became raspy and tight.

"Life got pretty bad with him, didn't it?"

"Yeah, but I'm thankful that I'm still alive. The last fight we had was the night I intended on telling him about the baby." She pressed her lips together, remembering the feel of his hands around her throat.

"You don't have to explain anything to me, but if you want to talk about it, you can."

"It's like poison in my system."

"Get it out if you need to."

"That night, I wanted to tell him about the baby. I hoped that maybe the baby would calm him down and he wouldn't hurt me anymore." She paused to catch her breath. "He didn't want to talk to me. He had friends coming over later and went out to the garage. I followed to see if he would at least come eat and talk while he ate, but I tripped on his toolbox he had sitting on the floor and grabbed for something to stop my fall. Unfortunately, I grabbed one of his totes and spilled it all over the garage floor." She remembered the rage on his face and shivered. "He put his hands around my throat, only letting me go before I passed out. The next day I left, taking the duffle bag with me."

"He was a despicable man," Roman mumbled, a dark shadow crossing his face, and his knuckles white on the steering wheel.

"I didn't tell anyone after that about the baby. I was too afraid to."

"You didn't do anything wrong. Nick was pure evil. Just know that I love you, and I'll always take care of you and the baby."

Reaching over, she caressed his bearded face. "I love you, too."

Chapter Thirty-Two

Hill picked them up at the rental agency. Roman ran around to the driver's side, but before Hill climbed into the back seat, Sophia stopped him.

"Please let me ride in the back. I want to rest." Hill nodded, and they buckled up for the four-hour ride to Atlanta. Sophia felt a black cloud had been lifted after talking to Roman, but she vowed not to talk of it again unless he asked. Feeling good, but tired, she dozed off in the back seat while the two men talked. When she woke up, they were only an hour outside of Atlanta.

"Roman, can we stop for a break and get something to eat?" she asked, rubbing her eyes.

"Yeah. I can use one, too."

"There are a few restaurants off the next exit." Hill pointed to the road sign just ahead. After a quick meal and a gas fill-up, they were on the interstate again. Before long, she saw a massive, ornate church and knew that Atlanta was just a few miles ahead. A semi-truck pulled ahead of them, blocking her view of the city, but soon the trucker changed lanes again, giving her a full panoramic view of the majestic skyscrapers.

"Hill, can you look up the address?" Roman asked, handing him the slip of paper.

"Yeah." Hill typed in the address to his phone. Sophia caught the look of surprise on his face.

"What is it? What is the location?" Sophia asked.

"The MARTA train station," Hill said in disbelief.

"A train station? Did you put in the right address?" She looked puzzled.

"Yeah." He held his phone up for her to see.

"I should have known it wasn't a bank," Roman said and explained. "Train stations have lockers you can rent for cash."

"So, it's a locker key," Sophia cried out.

"Yeah, and what better place to hide something? Throngs of people around, but no one paying any attention to what you're doing," Hill responded.

"And since the lockers are privately owned and rented out, it would be almost impossible to get a duplicate key," Roman explained, glancing back at Sophia in the rearview mirror.

"Ain't that the truth? You pay a small monthly fee into a cash machine, so it would be difficult to contact someone about the key," Hill added and shook his head.

"Now I understand Nick's determination to get the key. But what could be in the locker?" Sophia tried to hide the anguish in her voice. If he had been able to get a duplicate, how many people would still be alive?

"Money," Hill offered.

"Whatever it is, the police will need to be contacted," Roman reminded them.

"Let's go," Sophia said and silently prayed that the locker would be empty, but her gut told her otherwise.

As they neared downtown, Sophia looked up at the tall buildings, awed at their magnificence. When she spotted the Ambridge Hotel, she recalled Nick taking her there once and riding the outside elevator to the top. She had been terrified of the height, but the view of the setting sun had been breathtaking. Of course, that had been before the days of nasty Nick.

Feeling a quick swerve and then the screeching halt of the car and horns blowing long and loud behind them, Sophia grabbed for the door handle. Focusing on Roman, she saw him muttering under his breath, words that she probably didn't want to hear. Hill glanced back at her, biting his thumb nail, but his eyes were twinkling. With a quick smile, he faced the front again.

"Sorry if I scared you," Roman called out to her. "But we're in congested traffic, and some idiot pulled his car over in this lane toward the blue van in front of us." He smacked the steering wheel in frustration.

Another fifteen minutes found them in the crowded parking lot of the two-story train station. Three sliding glass doors were situated in the front, offering entrance and exit access for the mass of people coming and going. A two-lane drive curved in front to allow for easy drop-off and pickup of passengers, and the tracks were located behind the brick building.

Searching around, Roman took the ticket that was spit out at him and parked in the short-term parking lot. "Got the key?" he asked, shutting off the Charger and slipping his car keys in his pocket.

"Right here." Sophia patted her jacket pocket.

****

The train station was swarming with travelers moving in different directions with the five o'clock rush hour. Taking Sophia's hand, Roman pushed his way through the crowds, looking for the lockers, shielding her the best he could, with Hill behind her. He stopped short at a food bar, causing Hill to run into her.

"Sorry," he mumbled, scanning the area.

"There's a set of lockers by the women's restroom." Roman pointed to his right. Forcing their way through a throng of college students, they emerged at the lockers, searching for 105.

"I don't see it," Roman exclaimed, still looking over the six rows of gray lockers.

"I don't either." Sophia sighed, disappointed.

"I guess it could be another station, but this was the address," Roman said more to himself than to the others.

"Excuse me." A woman with a blue bandanna around her head tapped Sophia's shoulder as she tried to exit the bathroom. She was pushing a mop and a yellow bucket on wheels with sloshing brown water in it. Sophia moved away from the door.

"Excuse me, ma'am." Roman moved to the attendant's side. "Are these the only lockers in the station?"

"No. There's another set on the second level." The attendant pointed upward. Looking at Sophia she continued, "There's an elevator just around the corner here and past the banner advertising the zoo."

"Thanks." Roman grabbed Sophia's hand again, hurrying toward the elevator.

Once they were on the second level, the lockers were easier to spot. The mob of people was smaller than on the lower level. Hunting for 105, they found it quickly on the first row. Taking the key from her pocket, she handed it to Roman.

Twisting the bottom of the jacket between her fingers, she watched anxiously as Roman turned the key in the lock. Were they finally going to see what Nick had killed over? The door swung open. Inside were three large envelopes, stuffed full. Locking it back up, Roman suggested they leave and find somewhere private to inspect the contents.

"Where do you think we should go?" Sophia asked.

"What about getting a hotel room and going through them there?" Roman asked.

"Fine by me." Sophia nodded, looking up at Hill.

"I've got nowhere else to be." He shrugged, falling back behind Sophia as they waded through the crowds and back into the parking area.

Once in the car, Roman handed Sophia the envelopes. They were every bit as heavy as they looked. After passing Turner Field, Roman found a Holiday Inn and secured two rooms.

Sophia had laid the envelopes on the bed when they entered the room, and now the three stared at them as if they were snakes. Reaching down, Sophia picked one up and handed it to Roman.

"You do it. I can't." She and Hill sat down on the bed opposite Roman.

Taking the envelope, he ripped open the flap and pulled out a bundle of papers that had been divided and paper clipped into sections. Laying the envelope aside, he began reading and shifting through the papers. As he read, he frowned, occasionally glancing up at Sophia.

Again, Sophia wondered what was so important about those papers that Nick had killed for them, but she knew it would not be good. She hoped her baby was nothing like his father. With a light giddiness, she realized she was thinking of it being a boy. She raised her hand to her mouth and smiled briefly behind it, continuing to watch Roman.

One after another, Roman read the documents of the first envelope. The second and third envelopes, he looked into and then closed them back up. She thought she would explode with curiosity but remained silent until Roman was finished.

Finally, Roman rubbed his eyes and scooted Hill off the bed, then sat down beside her. She tensed up.

Roman exhaled slowly. "I don't know how to tell you this, Sophia, but it's beyond bad. It's horrifying."

"Roman, just please tell me."

"These papers are life insurance policies."

"Life insurance policies?" She frowned, not understanding.

"You told me your parents died in a car accident."

"Yeah."

"Has anyone ever told you what happened exactly?"

"The police thought Dad lost control and went over an embankment. I assumed he was drunk since a bottle of whiskey was found in his car. Why?"

"Nick was taking out life insurance policies on people and then collecting when they died. He probably killed them, which is why he needed to get the key to the locker and retrieve the evidence before anyone found it, namely you." He paused and took her hand. "There's a policy on each of your parents, with Nick as the beneficiary."

"What the...?" Hill rose to his feet, striding over to the window. "Damn!"

Sophia looked at Roman incredulously, shaking her head, her brows furrowed.

"Sophia, there are five policies in the envelope that Nick is the beneficiary of. One is a Teresa Sword, there is one on a Howard Sanders—"

"That's Casey's stepdad," Sophia interrupted in a shrill voice, staring wide-eyed at Roman.

"There's one on each of your parents, and there's one on you," Roman finished and took her cold hands in his, giving her time to absorb the information. "Sophia, you're the only one without a death certificate."

"Oh, God! Nick killed my parents!" Sophia screamed out, the realization punching her in the gut. Tears spilled forth as she rocked back and forth, wringing her hands and screaming over and over until Roman pulled her tightly into his arms, caressing her long hair. When she was calmer, he pulled back from her.

"At this point, this is merely speculation, but it seems pretty clear to me. The other two envelopes are filled with money. Probably the insurance money."

"Roman, I got my parents killed. If I had only listened to them and not married Nick…" She squealed. Her shrill voice trailed off as fresh tears spilled down her cheeks. Hill handed her a box of tissues and knelt beside her.

"You didn't get your parents killed. Nick used you. Roman is right. He was viciously evil," Hill said.

"He was going to kill me, too," she cried, wiping her face with the tissue.

"Do you know who this Teresa Sword is?"

"I found a picture of a woman tucked away in a drawer. When I asked who she was he told me Teresa and she was his ex-girlfriend. He said she ran off with some man to Virginia." She sniffed.

"Hill, if you'll call the sheriff, I'll call Uncle Ralph."

Hill nodded. "By the way, how much money do you think is in there?" he asked Roman. Roman curled his lip up and shook his head.

"By my rough estimate, a little over three hundred

thousand. It will have to be surrendered to the police."

"Too bad for Sophia. That could have helped her a lot." Hill sighed and made his phone call, pulling back the curtain to stare out at the city when he hung up.

Sophia sat on the bed and listened to Roman explain everything to Mr. Danes. How many more people died because of the money in those envelopes? Blood money.

Roman finished his call. "Hill, is the sheriff on his way?"

"Yeah." Hill let the drapes fall back in place. "I'll go down and meet him. I want a drink from the machine in the lobby anyway."

"I'll go with you." Roman stood up. "Sophia, do you want to go down or can I bring you something to drink."

"A Sprite."

"Okay, we'll be back." Both men left the room, leaving her to her thoughts.

Chapter Thirty-Three

"Sophia," Roman's voice called out. She heard him set the can on the table.

"I'm in the bathroom," she called out, rinsing her face, but her eyes were still puffy. She emerged, the shock from the dark twisting deeds of earlier beginning to fade. "Where's Hill?"

"He's coming up with the sheriff." Roman reached out and pulled her to him. She laid her cheek against his chest until he leaned over, lifted her chin and kissed her. He laid her gently on the bed, his kisses and soft caresses erasing the weariness from her exhausted body. Unfortunately, the moment was fleeting. There was a rap on the door.

"Police." Roman went to the door while Sophia got up off the bed and moved to the window, smoothing her hair down. A sheriff and two detectives strode professionally into the room, followed by Hill.

"Hello, Sophia, I'm Sheriff Carson, and these two men are my detectives, Martin and Curtis. We need to question you, but I promise we'll be as brief as we can."

"Okay." She glanced at Roman as Martin began to take pictures of the envelopes, the money, and the note.

"I'll be right here. They know that I'm your attorney." Nodding, she sat down at the table. Detective Curtis sat opposite her, staring with cold brown eyes.

For forty-five minutes, her emotions yo-yoed as the sheriff and Detective Curtis grilled her about Nick and Casey while she told them everything she could remember. When they asked her about Nick's prior girlfriend, Teresa Sword, Sophia shook her head. She had very little information about her.

"Thank you for your help." Sheriff Carson shook Sophia's hand after Detective Martin had everything bagged and tagged. "We'll try to contact Teresa's family and exhume her body."

"I don't think she had any family, according to Nick."

"We'll see." The sheriff opened the door, but Curtis paused and stared back at Sophia.

"One more question." Sophia nodded impatiently, ready for them to leave.

"Nick's parents died also?"

"In a car accident, he said."

"So, you didn't know that until June of last year his mother was living in Texas or that his dad was in prison in Louisiana."

Sophia bristled. "No, I thought his parents were dead."

"They are now. His mom died of cancer last June. His dad died in prison of a heart attack a year before that." Curtis turned and left the room.

"Please, Roman, no more police."

"See what I can do." He reached for her. She drifted into his arms, losing herself in his embrace.

"Well, this is awkward," Hill announced, emerging from the bathroom. "I'll just mosey on over to my room." He left chuckling.

Roman kissed her again. "Sophia, sit down and

close your eyes."

"What?"

"Humor me."

Sophia sat on the bed wondering what Roman was up to. She could hear him shuffling around but kept her eyes shut tight.

"Open your eyes." Her face lit up in surprise. He was on his knees in front of her, his eyes twinkling, holding out a small silver box to her. She lifted the lid and gasped. A princess-cut diamond ring glimmered in the box. She gazed into his blue eyes, her heart swelling with love.

"I know this has been a horrifying day for you, with finding out about the policies and the money, but I want to tell you that I love you. I want to spend my life with you and the baby."

"Oh, Roman."

"Will you marry me, Sophia?"

"Yes, I will," she exclaimed, as he slipped the ring on her finger.

****

When the sun rose over Atlanta the next morning, Sophia, Roman, and Hill left the city behind.

"What happens now?" Sophia asked.

"There will be an official inquest, and you for sure will have to give testimony again. Uncle Ralph will explain more in detail, but I want you to be prepared for the police wanting to exhume your parents' bodies. Their car will be investigated also, if it can be found."

She frowned slightly. She had hoped it wouldn't come to that, but obviously it would have to be done. "Will all this ever be over?"

Reaching over the console, Roman squeezed her

hand. "It will be. I promise."

"Have you told Hill our news?" she asked.

"No. You tell him, or better yet, show him." Sophia, filled with happiness, held up her left hand to show him the sparkling ring on her finger.

"Hey congrats, buddy!" Hill laughed out loud. "Although it's not too much of a surprise."

Chapter Thirty-Four

Relaxed on the sofa in her new house, Sophia sat with her legs curled under her, cuddling her baby in her arms. An intense love for the child filled her as he cooed and waved his tiny hands in the air. Max, their large black Lab, lay beside them, his head on her leg, but he leaped off the sofa when the doorbell rang, his tail wagging excitedly.

"I'll get it," Roman called out, coming down the stairs. He opened the door to a warm spring day, and Sophia heard a familiar voice bellow out when Mr. and Mrs. Danes entered the room.

"Where's that baby boy?" Mr. Danes asked, reaching down to scratch Max's head.

"I hope that precious baby's not sleeping." Mrs. Danes moved toward the sofa, her lips curved in a gentle smile.

"No, he's awake." Sophia beckoned her to sit beside them. Mrs. Danes was a slim, petite woman with silver hair and a soft, quiet personality. Her blue eyes lit up whenever she was around the baby. When she was beside her, Sophia passed the baby to her. Only then did she see the two men that had followed Mr. Danes into the house. One was Detective Martin, but the other was unknown to her.

"A beautiful child. What's his name?" the unknown

man asked. She took note of his black-rimmed glasses and dark suit with the blue striped bow tie.

"Lucas Michael." Sophia looked inquiringly at Roman.

"They need to speak with you."

Nodding, she told Mrs. Danes, who was chattering with Lucas, that she would be back and followed the men to the kitchen and sat at the table.

Detective Martin drew out his notebook from his jacket pocket. "I'll go first." Drawing a deep breath, he consulted his notes and continued. "Teresa's death was reported as an accidental drowning caused by her consumption of too much alcohol. In the autopsy, trace amounts of alcohol were found, but the coroner also found some bruising of shoulder tissue indicative of someone holding her down."

"So, she was murdered. How long ago did she die?" Roman asked, standing behind Sophia.

"Eighteen months, according to the coroner."

Sophia gasped audibly. "That was just a couple of months before we met."

"And Teresa and Nick were married," Detective Martin added.

"How horrible." Sophia gasped again and looked away, saddened for Teresa. How much longer would she have lived if she hadn't left when she did?

"Sophia, I also have the report on your parents' exhumation," Martin continued.

"I'm ready." She tensed up, grasping the edge of the table.

"Their death was caused from injuries sustained in the accident." Sophia nodded. "Although there was a bottle of alcohol found in the car, there was no alcohol found in your dad's tissues."

"Oh," Sophia exclaimed, her heart breaking. All this time she thought he had been drunk.

"We also tracked the car to Denny's Junkyard. CSI scoured the car. Not much was found, except for a fingerprint on the headrest of the driver's seat. It belonged to Casey."

"What?" Sophia cried out, bewildered. "Casey?"

"Yes."

"So, he killed my parents?" Stunned, she inhaled deeply, her pulse quickening as she twisted the hem of her shirt around her fingers. Roman stroked her shoulder gently.

"We don't know yet what happened or how he got out of the car before it went over the embankment."

Sophia mused silently over the information, letting it sink in. Her poor, sweet parents terrorized by that vile man. Right or wrong, she felt Casey had gotten what he deserved. Closing her eyes, she visualized her parents the last time she saw them. Then with her jaw set she rose from her chair. "Is that all?"

"Yes, so I'll leave now. Hope everything goes well for you two. I can find my way out." He shook hands with Sophia and left. Sophia turned to the man in the suit.

"I guess it's your turn."

The man pulled a long white envelope from his suit coat pocket. "Mrs. Danes, my name is James Castle, and I work for Martenal Insurance Company out of Knoxville." With a sinking feeling, Sophia glanced over at Roman, but couldn't read his face. Moving closer to him, she slipped her hand in his and nodded for Mr. Castle to continue.

"Mr. Ralph Danes has informed me that the inquest

is over, and everything has been settled. I am sorry to hear about your parents' death, but they did have life insurance policies. Not the policies Nick had, but ones they bought, naming you the beneficiary. So, I'm delivering you a check today in the amount of one hundred thousand dollars." He finished by pushing the envelope across the table to her. "And if I may say so, I found your father to be a good humored, cheery man, and he was very proud of you."

"Thank you, Mr. Castle," she replied, taking it all in. She took the envelope and held it up. "Roman?"

"Uncle Ralph uncovered the policies during the investigation and made all the arrangements for you to get the benefits."

"Thank you, Mr. Danes!" Sophia rushed over and threw her arms around the big man's neck.

"Sophia, call me Uncle Ralph!" he said, laughing out loud.

"Uncle Ralph it is."

A word about the author…

Lynne lives in Tennessee. She plays piano and loves to read most any genre. She enjoys old-time rock and roll music, especially Elvis. She's always up for adventures and exploring places she's never been to, while looking for new ideas to write about.

Visit her at:

https://www.facebook.com/lynne.h.conrad